THE SMURF KING

Peyo

THE SMURF KING

It's disgraceful! A scandal! What bunch of smurfs dared to smurf that?
It's the rebels!
REVOLT, SMURFS
DOWN WITH THE S
DON'T LET YOURSELF BE SMURFED ANY LONGER!
HURRAH FOR LIBERTY!
THE SMURF KING IS A
SMURF WITH

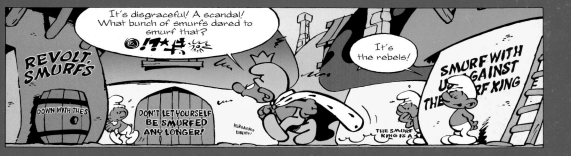

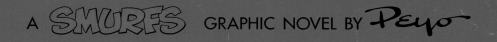

A SMURFS GRAPHIC NOVEL BY PEYO

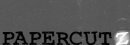

PAPERCUTZ™
NEW YORK

SMURFS GRAPHIC NOVELS AVAILABLE FROM PAPERCUTZ™

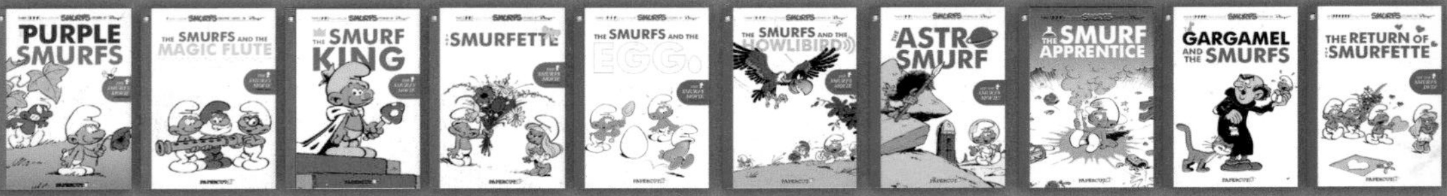
PURPLE SMURFS
THE SMURFS AND THE MAGIC FLUTE
THE SMURF KING
SMURFETTE
THE SMURFS AND THE EGG
THE SMURFS AND THE HOWLIBIRD
THE ASTRO SMURF
THE SMURF APPRENTICE
GARGAMEL AND THE SMURFS
THE RETURN OF THE SMURFETTE

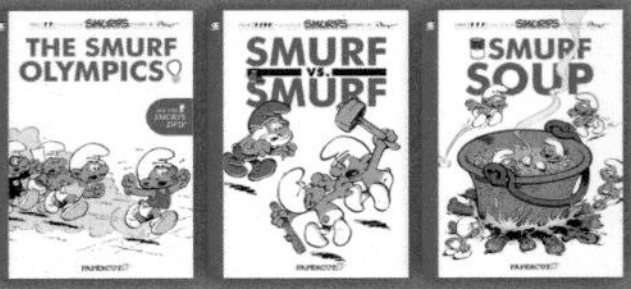
THE SMURF OLYMPICS
SMURF VS. SMURF
SMURF SOUP

1. THE PURPLE SMURFS
2. THE SMURFS AND THE MAGIC FLUTE
3. THE SMURF KING
4. THE SMURFETTE
5. THE SMURFS AND THE EGG
6. THE SMURFS AND THE HOWLIBIRD
7. THE ASTROSMURF
8. THE SMURF APPRENTICE
9. GARGAMEL AND THE SMURFS
10. THE RETURN OF THE SMURFETTE
11. THE SMURF OLYMPICS
12. SMURF VS. SMURF
13. SMURF SOUP

COMING SOON:

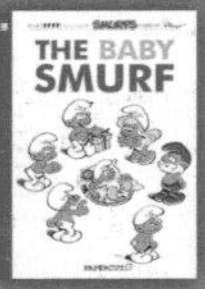
THE BABY SMURF

14. THE BABY SMURF

THE SMURFS graphic novels are available in paperback for $5.99 each and in hardcover for $10.99 each at booksellers everywhere. Or order from us. Please add $4.00 for postage and handling for the first book, add $1.00 for each additional book. Please make check payable to NBM Publishing. Send to: PAPERCUTZ, 160 Broadway, Suite 700, East Wing, New York, NY 10038 (1-800-886-1223)

THE SMURFS graphic novels are also available digitally from COMIXOLOGY.com.

WWW.PAPERCUTZ.COM

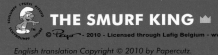

THE SMURF KING

"The Smurf King"
BY YVAN DELPORTE AND PEYO

"The Smurfony"
BY YVAN DELPORTE AND PEYO

Joe Johnson, *SMURFLATIONS*
Adam Grano, *SMURFIC DESIGN*
Janice Chiang, *LETTERING SMURFETTE*
Matt. Murray, *SMURF CONSULTANT*
Michael Petranek, *ASSOCIATE SMURF*
Jim Salicrup, *SMURF-IN-CHIEF*

PAPERBACK EDITION ISBN: 978-1-59707-224-3
HARDCOVER EDITION ISBN: 978-1-59707-225-0

PRINTED IN CHINA
OCTOBER 2012 BY WKT CO. LTD.
3/F PHASE 1 LEADER INDUSTRIAL CENTRE
188 TEXACO RD., TSUEN WAN, N.T., HONG KONG

DISTRIBUTED BY MACMILLAN
FIFTH PAPERCUTZ PRINTING

THE SMURF KING

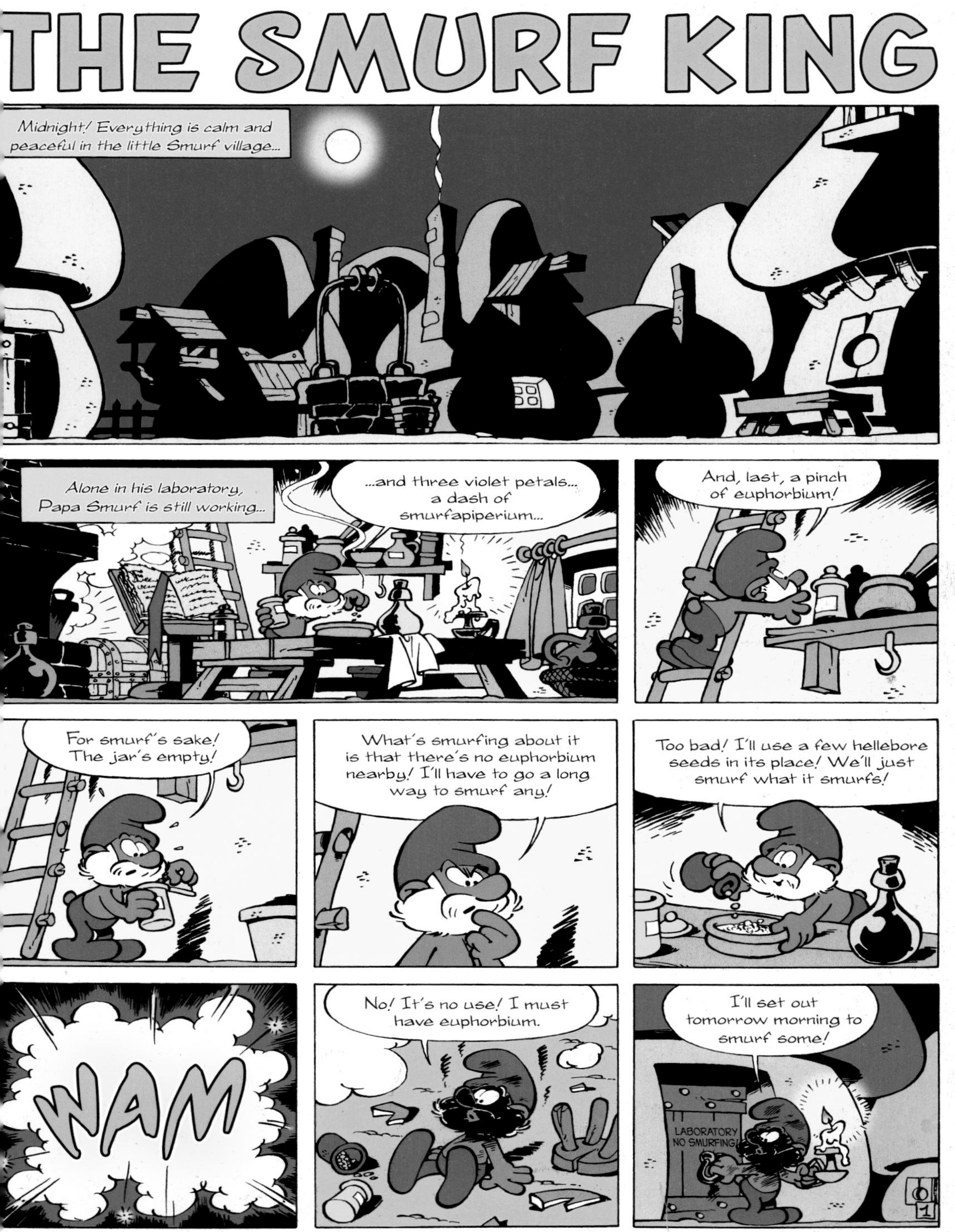
Midnight! Everything is calm and peaceful in the little Smurf village...
Alone in his laboratory, Papa Smurf is still working...
...and three violet petals... a dash of smurfapiperium...
And, last, a pinch of euphorbium!
For smurf's sake! The jar's empty!
What's smurfing about it is that there's no euphorbium nearby! I'll have to go a long way to smurf any!
Too bad! I'll use a few hellebore seeds in its place! We'll just smurf what it smurfs!
WAM
No! It's no use! I must have euphorbium.
I'll set out tomorrow morning to smurf some!
LABORATORY NO SMURFING!

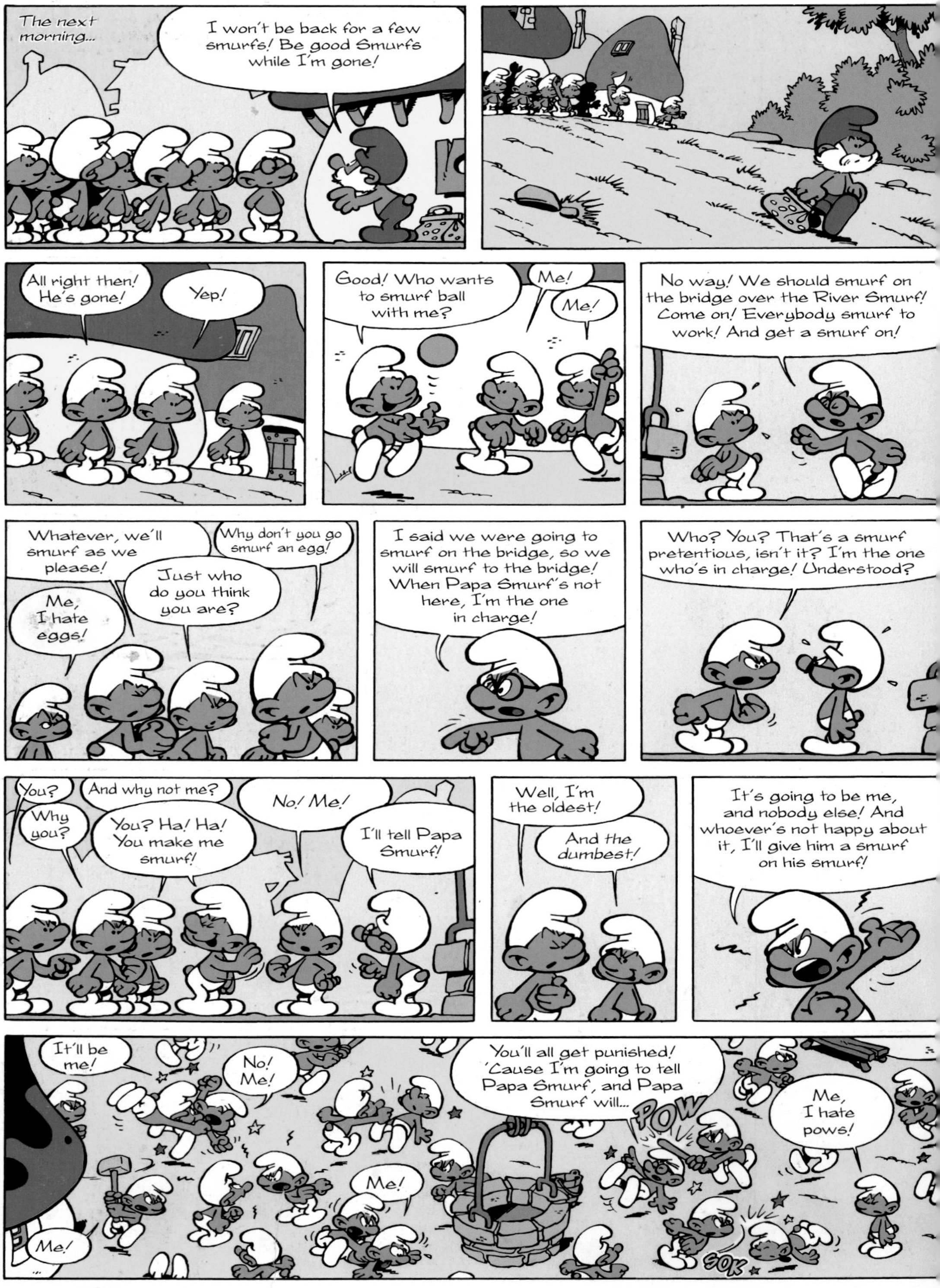
The next morning...
I won't be back for a few smurfs! Be good Smurfs while I'm gone!
All right then! He's gone!
Yep!
Good! Who wants to smurf ball with me?
Me!
Me!
No way! We should smurf on the bridge over the River Smurf! Come on! Everybody smurf to work! And get a smurf on!
Whatever, we'll smurf as we please!
Why don't you go smurf an egg!
Just who do you think you are?
Me, I hate eggs!
I said we were going to smurf on the bridge, so we will smurf to the bridge! When Papa Smurf's not here, I'm the one in charge!
Who? You? That's a smurf pretentious, isn't it? I'm the one who's in charge! Understood?
You?
And why not me?
Why you?
You? Ha! Ha! You make me smurf!
No! Me!
I'll tell Papa Smurf!
Well, I'm the oldest!
And the dumbest!
It's going to be me, and nobody else! And whoever's not happy about it, I'll give him a smurf on his smurf!
It'll be me!
No! Me!
You'll all get punished! 'Cause I'm going to tell Papa Smurf, and Papa Smurf will...
POW
Me, I hate pows!
Me!
Me!
SOK

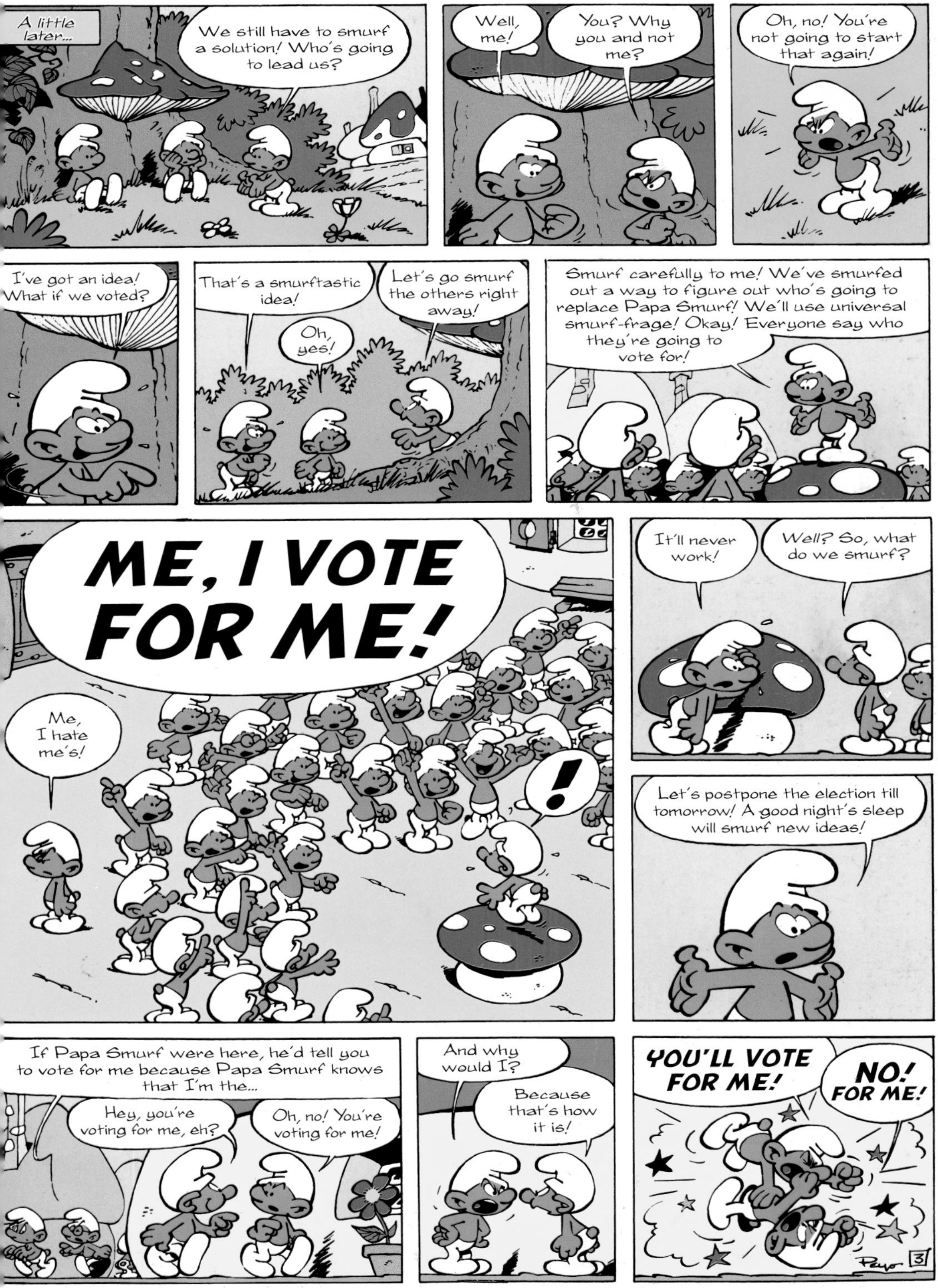
A little later...
We still have to smurf a solution! Who's going to lead us?
Well, me!
You? Why you and not me?
Oh, no! You're not going to start that again!
I've got an idea! What if we voted?
That's a smurftastic idea!
Oh, yes!
Let's go smurf the others right away!
Smurf carefully to me! We've smurfed out a way to figure out who's going to replace Papa Smurf! We'll use universal smurf-frage! Okay! Everyone say who they're going to vote for!
ME, I VOTE FOR ME!
Me, I hate me's!
!
It'll never work!
Well? So, what do we smurf?
Let's postpone the election till tomorrow! A good night's sleep will smurf new ideas!
If Papa Smurf were here, he'd tell you to vote for me because Papa Smurf knows that I'm the...
Hey, you're voting for me, eh?
Oh, no! You're voting for me!
And why would I?
Because that's how it is!
YOU'LL VOTE FOR ME!
NO! FOR ME!
Peyo
3

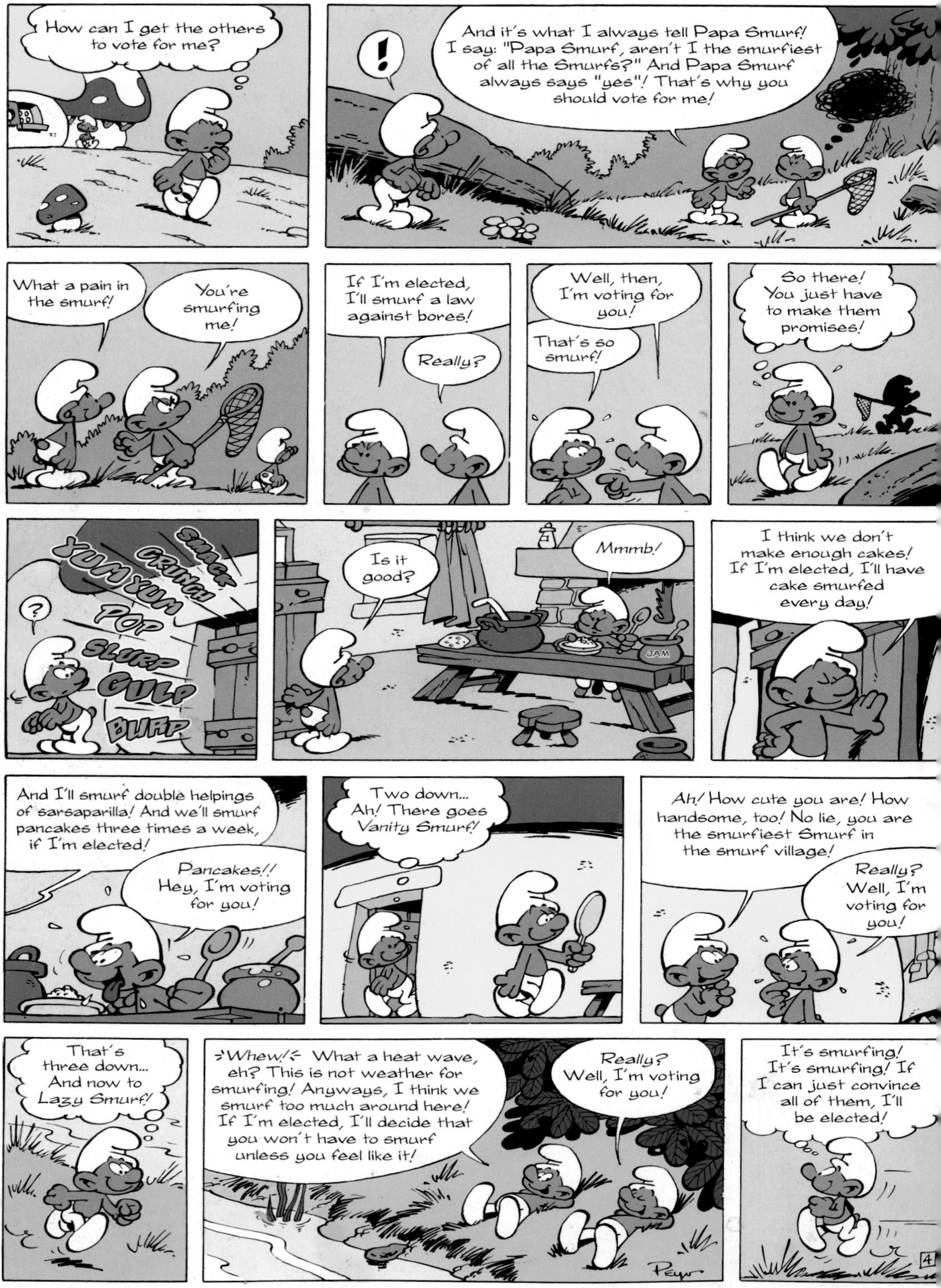
How can I get the others to vote for me?
!
And it's what I always tell Papa Smurf! I say: "Papa Smurf, aren't I the smurfiest of all the Smurfs?" And Papa Smurf always says "yes"! That's why you should vote for me!
What a pain in the smurf!
You're smurfing me!
If I'm elected, I'll smurf a law against bores!
Really?
Well, then, I'm voting for you!
That's so smurf!
So there! You just have to make them promises!
SMACK
CRUNCH
YUM YUM
POP
SLURP
GULP
BURP
?
Is it good?
Mmmb!
JAM
I think we don't make enough cakes! If I'm elected, I'll have cake smurfed every day!
And I'll smurf double helpings of sarsaparilla! And we'll smurf pancakes three times a week, if I'm elected!
Pancakes!! Hey, I'm voting for you!
Two down... Ah! There goes Vanity Smurf!
Ah! How cute you are! How handsome, too! No lie, you are the smurfiest Smurf in the smurf village!
Really? Well, I'm voting for you!
That's three down... And now to Lazy Smurf!
Whew! What a heat wave, eh? This is not weather for smurfing! Anyways, I think we smurf too much around here! If I'm elected, I'll decide that you won't have to smurf unless you feel like it!
Really? Well, I'm voting for you!
Peyo
It's smurfing! It's smurfing! If I can just convince all of them, I'll be elected!
4

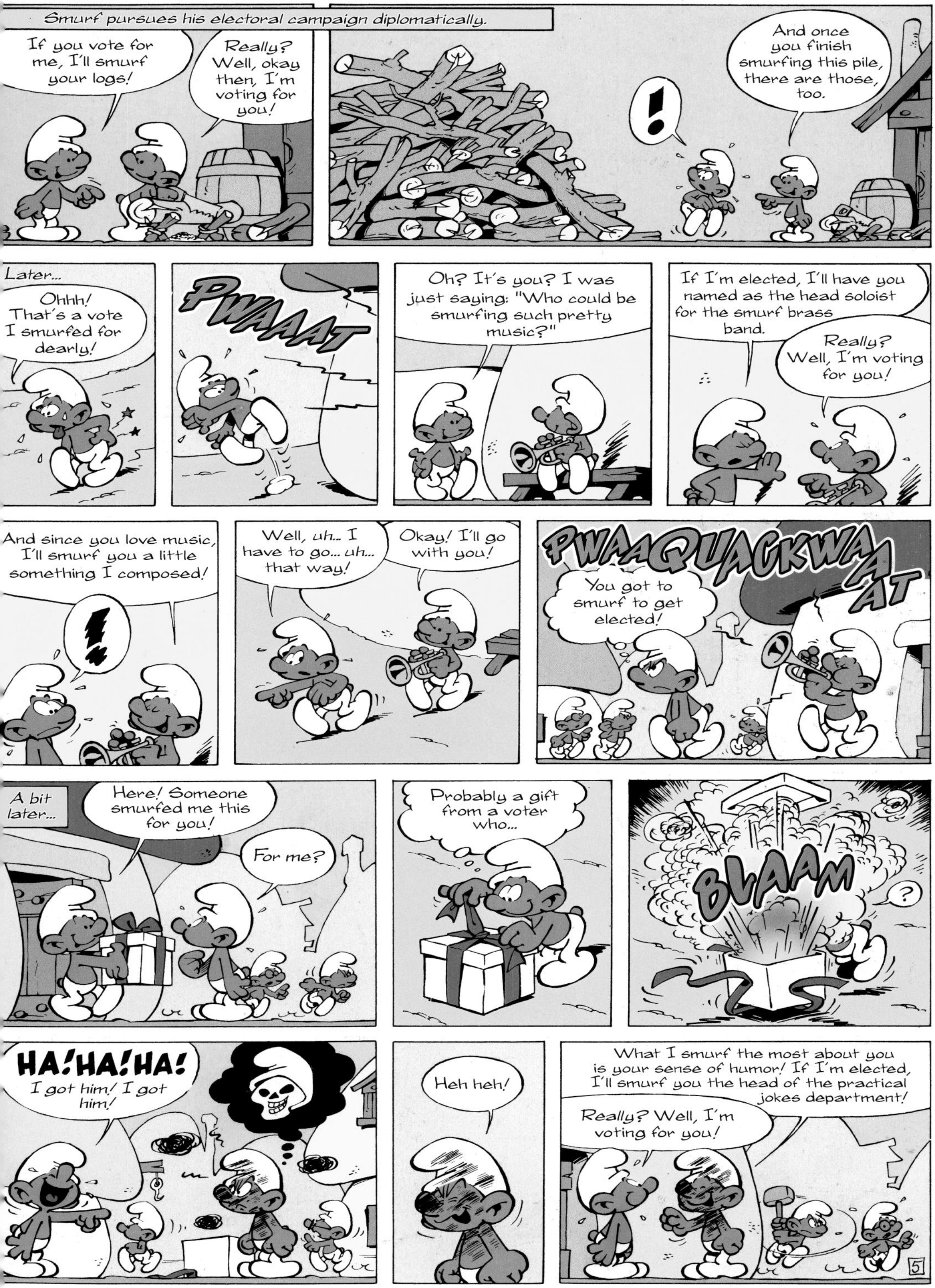
Smurf pursues his electoral campaign diplomatically.
If you vote for me, I'll smurf your logs!
Really? Well, okay then, I'm voting for you!
!
And once you finish smurfing this pile, there are those, too.
Later...
Ohhh! That's a vote I smurfed for dearly!
PWAAAT
Oh? It's you? I was just saying: "Who could be smurfing such pretty music?"
If I'm elected, I'll have you named as the head soloist for the smurf brass band.
Really? Well, I'm voting for you!
And since you love music, I'll smurf you a little something I composed!
Well, uh... I have to go... uh... that way!
Okay! I'll go with you!
PWAAQUACKWAAAT
You got to smurf to get elected!
A bit later...
Here! Someone smurfed me this for you!
For me?
Probably a gift from a voter who...
BLAAM
?
HA!HA!HA! I got him! I got him!
Heh heh!
What I smurf the most about you is your sense of humor! If I'm elected, I'll smurf you the head of the practical jokes department!
Really? Well, I'm voting for you!
5

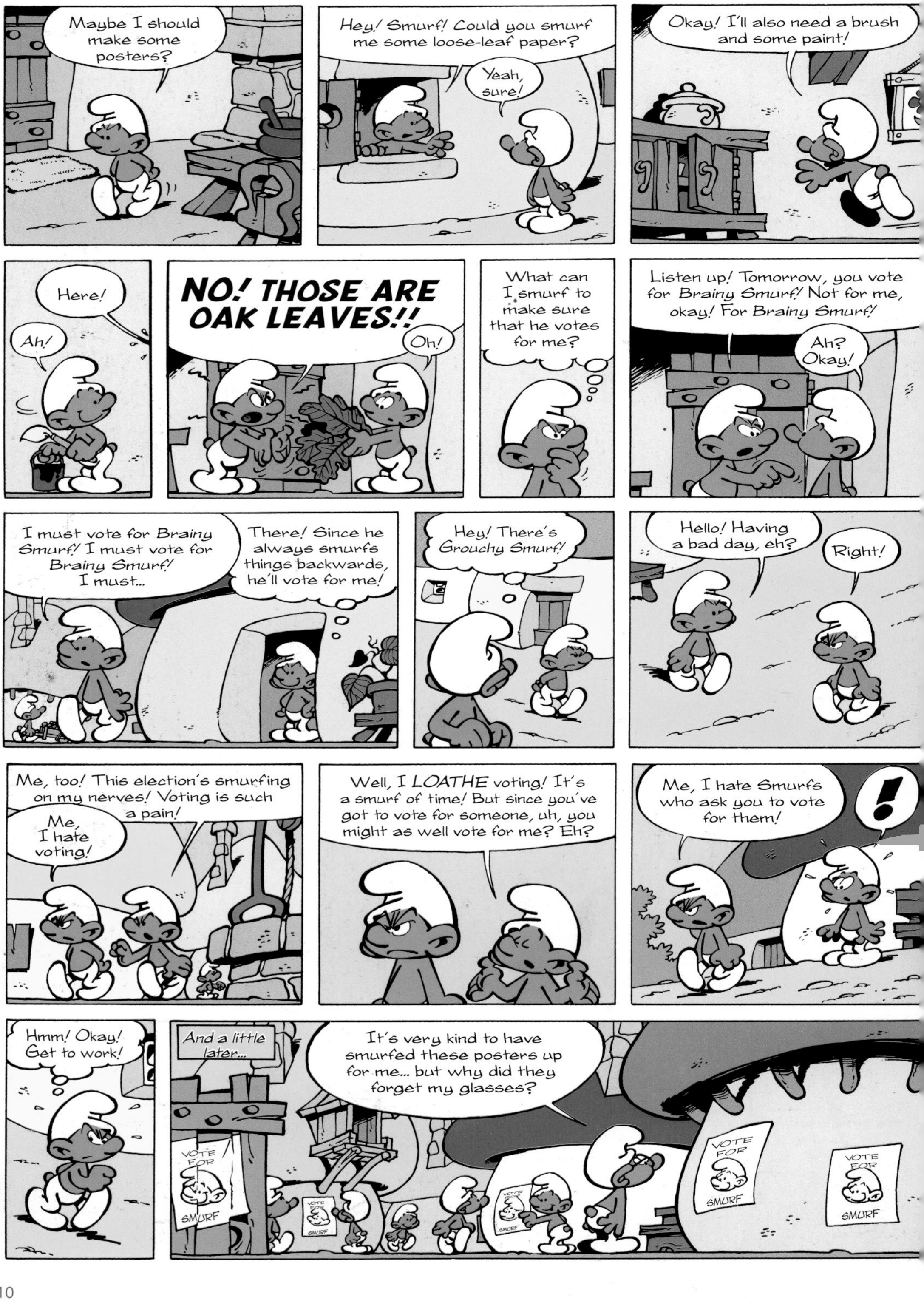

Maybe I should make some posters?
Hey! Smurf! Could you smurf me some loose-leaf paper?
Yeah, sure!
Okay! I'll also need a brush and some paint!
Here!
Ah!
NO! THOSE ARE OAK LEAVES!!
Oh!
What can I smurf to make sure that he votes for me?
Listen up! Tomorrow, you vote for Brainy Smurf! Not for me, okay! For Brainy Smurf!
Ah? Okay!
I must vote for Brainy Smurf! I must vote for Brainy Smurf! I must...
There! Since he always smurfs things backwards, he'll vote for me!
Hey! There's Grouchy Smurf!
Hello! Having a bad day, eh?
Right!
Me, too! This election's smurfing on my nerves! Voting is such a pain!
Me, I hate voting!
Well, I LOATHE voting! It's a smurf of time! But since you've got to vote for someone, uh, you might as well vote for me? Eh?
Me, I hate Smurfs who ask you to vote for them!
!
Hmm! Okay! Get to work!
And a little later...
It's very kind to have smurfed these posters up for me... but why did they forget my glasses?
VOTE FOR SMURF
VOTE FOR SMURF
VOTE FOR SMURF
VOTE FOR SMURF

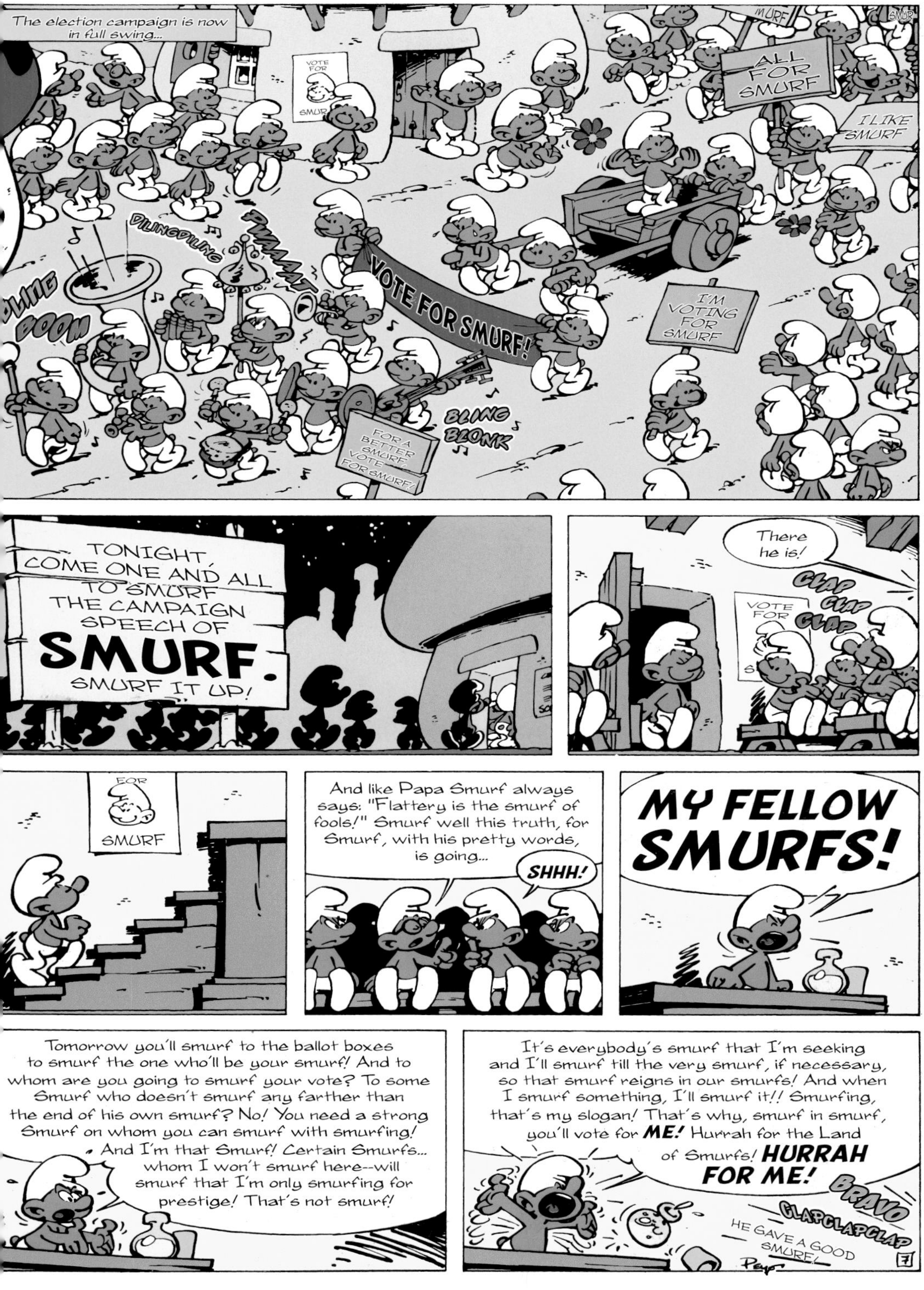

The election campaign is now in full swing...
VOTE FOR SMURF
ALL FOR SMURF
I LIKE SMURF
DILINGDILING
PWAAAAT
BOOM
VOTE FOR SMURF!
I'M VOTING FOR SMURF
BLING BLONK
FOR A BETTER SMURF VOTE FOR SMURF!
TONIGHT COME ONE AND ALL TO SMURF THE CAMPAIGN SPEECH OF SMURF. SMURF IT UP!
There he is!
CLAP CLAP CLAP
VOTE FOR
FOR
SMURF
And like Papa Smurf always says: "Flattery is the smurf of fools!" Smurf well this truth, for Smurf, with his pretty words, is going...
SHHH!
MY FELLOW SMURFS!
Tomorrow you'll smurf to the ballot boxes to smurf the one who'll be your smurf! And to whom are you going to smurf your vote? To some Smurf who doesn't smurf any farther than the end of his own smurf? No! You need a strong Smurf on whom you can smurf with smurfing! And I'm that Smurf! Certain Smurfs... whom I won't smurf here--will smurf that I'm only smurfing for prestige! That's not smurf!
It's everybody's smurf that I'm seeking and I'll smurf till the very smurf, if necessary, so that smurf reigns in our smurfs! And when I smurf something, I'll smurf it!! Smurfing, that's my slogan! That's why, smurf in smurf, you'll vote for ME! Hurrah for the Land of Smurfs! HURRAH FOR ME!
BRAVO
CLAPCLAPCLAP
HE GAVE A GOOD SMURF!
Peyo
7

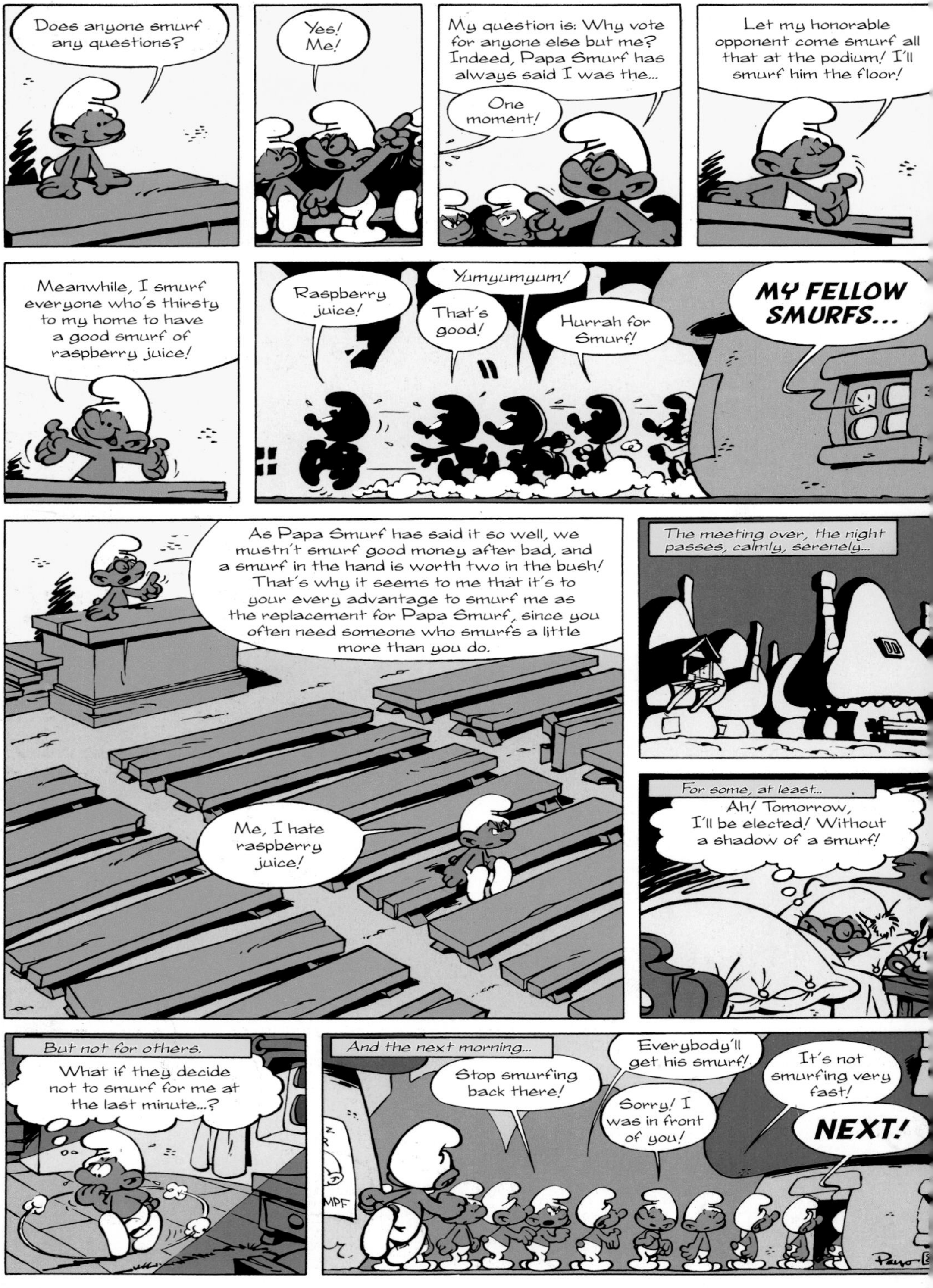

Does anyone smurf any questions?
Yes! Me!
My question is: Why vote for anyone else but me? Indeed, Papa Smurf has always said I was the...
One moment!
Let my honorable opponent come smurf all that at the podium! I'll smurf him the floor!
Meanwhile, I smurf everyone who's thirsty to my home to have a good smurf of raspberry juice!
Raspberry juice!
Yumyumyum!
That's good!
Hurrah for Smurf!
MY FELLOW SMURFS...
As Papa Smurf has said it so well, we mustn't smurf good money after bad, and a smurf in the hand is worth two in the bush! That's why it seems to me that it's to your every advantage to smurf me as the replacement for Papa Smurf, since you often need someone who smurfs a little more than you do.
Me, I hate raspberry juice!
The meeting over, the night passes, calmly, serenely...
For some, at least...
Ah! Tomorrow, I'll be elected! Without a shadow of a smurf!
But not for others.
What if they decide not to smurf for me at the last minute...?
And the next morning...
Stop smurfing back there!
Everybody'll get his smurf!
Sorry! I was in front of you!
It's not smurfing very fast!
NEXT!

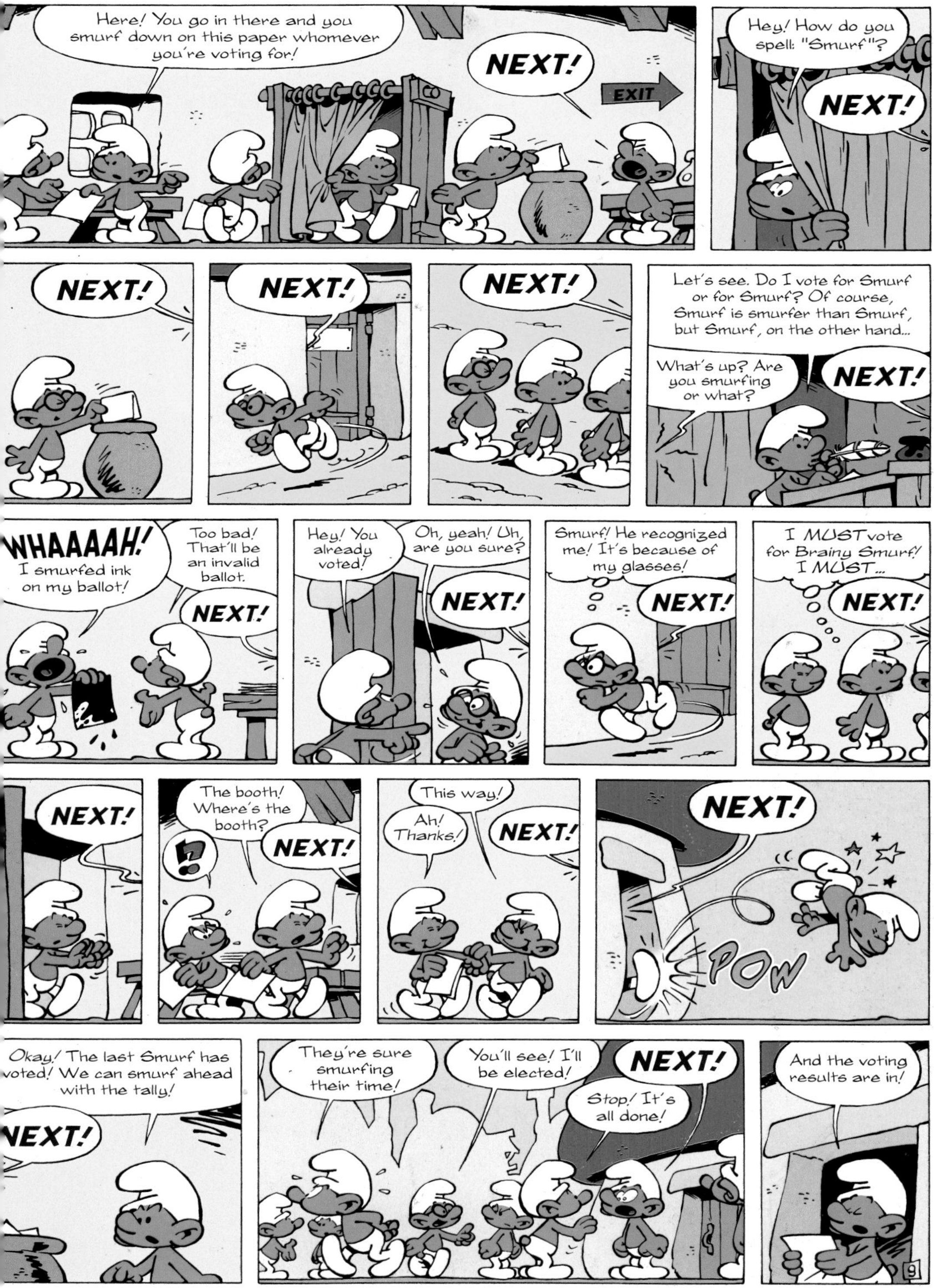

Here! You go in there and you smurf down on this paper whomever you're voting for!
NEXT!
EXIT
Hey! How do you spell: "Smurf"?
NEXT!
NEXT!
NEXT!
NEXT!
Let's see. Do I vote for Smurf or for Smurf? Of course, Smurf is smurfer than Smurf, but Smurf, on the other hand...
What's up? Are you smurfing or what?
NEXT!
WHAAAAH! I smurfed ink on my ballot!
Too bad! That'll be an invalid ballot.
NEXT!
Hey! You already voted!
Oh, yeah! Uh, are you sure?
NEXT!
Smurf! He recognized me! It's because of my glasses!
NEXT!
I MUST vote for Brainy Smurf! I MUST...
NEXT!
NEXT!
The booth! Where's the booth?
NEXT!
This way!
Ah! Thanks!
NEXT!
NEXT!
POW
Okay! The last Smurf has voted! We can smurf ahead with the tally!
NEXT!
They're sure smurfing their time!
You'll see! I'll be elected!
NEXT!
Stop! It's all done!
And the voting results are in!
9

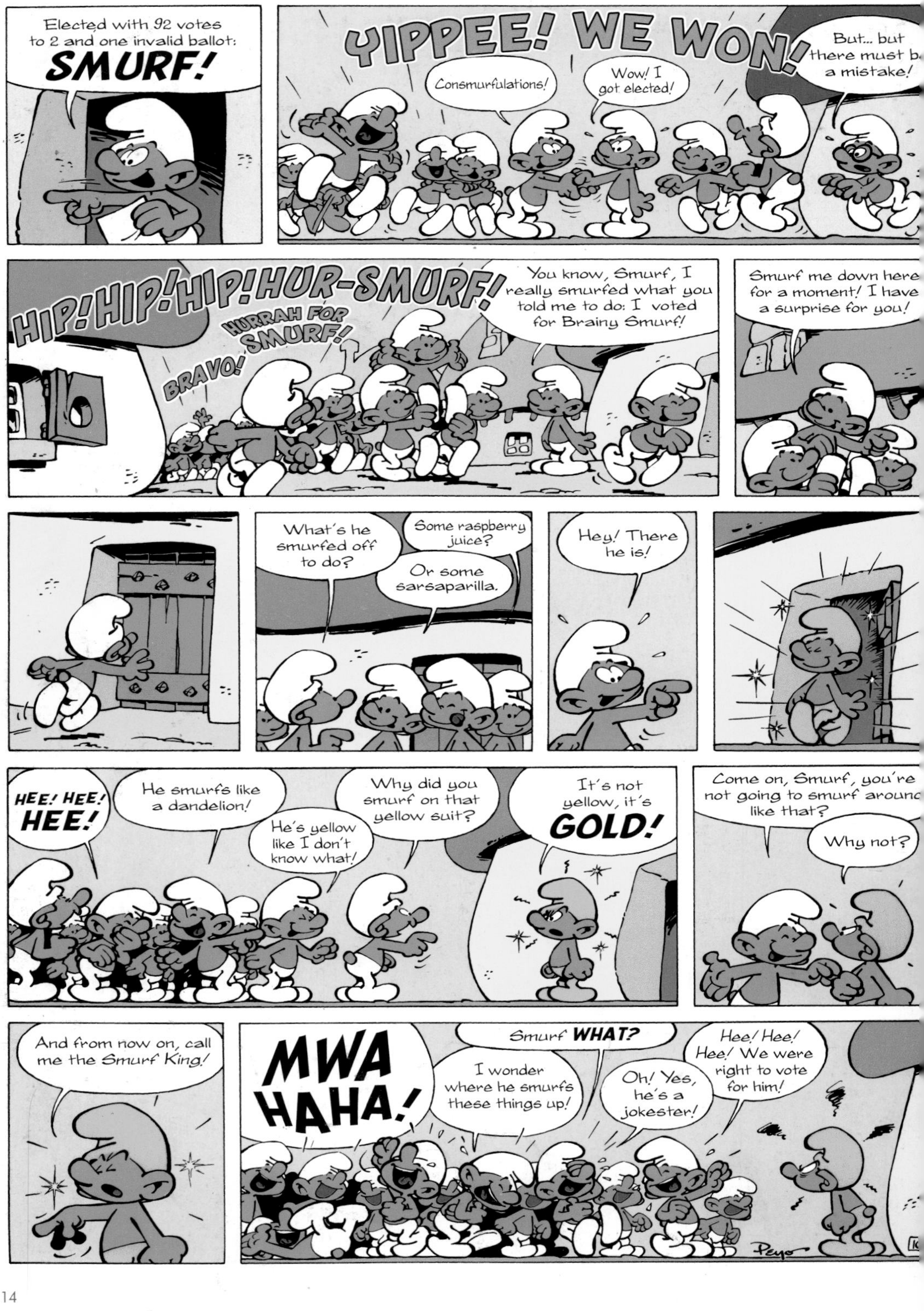

Elected with 92 votes to 2 and one invalid ballot:
SMURF!
YIPPEE! WE WON!
Consmurfulations!
Wow! I got elected!
But... but there must b a mistake!
HIP! HIP! HIP! HUR-SMURF!
HURRAH FOR SMURF!
BRAVO!
You know, Smurf, I really smurfed what you told me to do: I voted for Brainy Smurf!
Smurf me down here for a moment! I have a surprise for you!
What's he smurfed off to do?
Some raspberry juice?
Or some sarsaparilla.
Hey! There he is!
HEE! HEE! HEE!
He smurfs like a dandelion!
He's yellow like I don't know what!
Why did you smurf on that yellow suit?
It's not yellow, it's GOLD!
Come on, Smurf, you're not going to smurf around like that?
Why not?
And from now on, call me the Smurf King!
MWA HAHA!
Smurf WHAT?
I wonder where he smurfs these things up!
Oh! Yes, he's a jokester!
Hee! Hee! Hee! We were right to vote for him!
Peyo

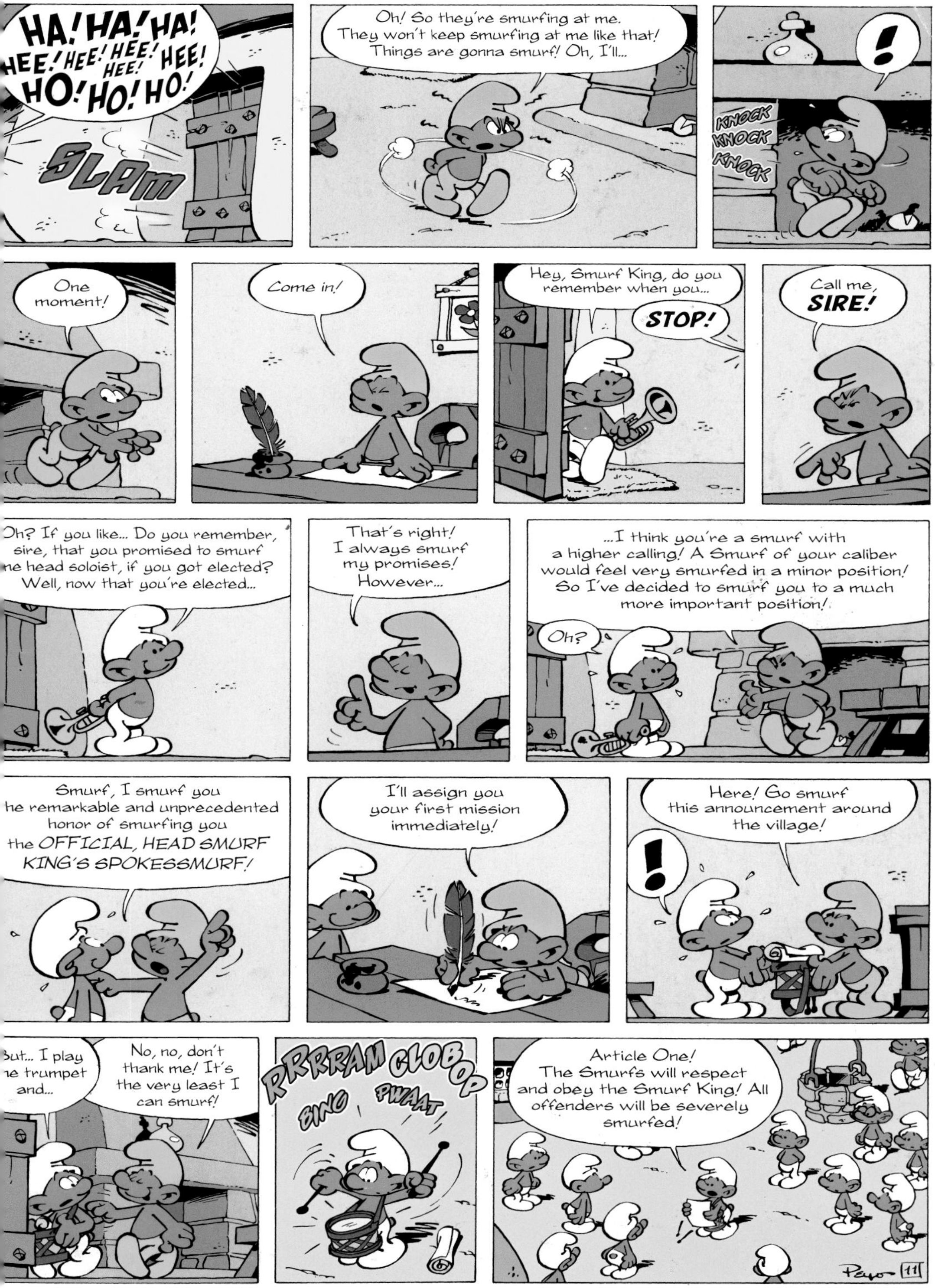
HA! HA! HA! HEE! HEE! HEE! HEE! HEE! HO! HO! HO!
SLAM
Oh! So they're smurfing at me. They won't keep smurfing at me like that! Things are gonna smurf! Oh, I'll...
KNOCK KNOCK KNOCK
!
One moment!
Come in!
Hey, Smurf King, do you remember when you...
STOP!
Call me, SIRE!
Oh? If you like... Do you remember, sire, that you promised to smurf me head soloist, if you got elected? Well, now that you're elected...
That's right! I always smurf my promises! However...
...I think you're a smurf with a higher calling! A Smurf of your caliber would feel very smurfed in a minor position! So I've decided to smurf you to a much more important position!
Oh?
Smurf, I smurf you the remarkable and unprecedented honor of smurfing you the OFFICIAL, HEAD SMURF KING'S SPOKESSMURF!
I'll assign you your first mission immediately!
Here! Go smurf this announcement around the village!
!
But... I play the trumpet and...
No, no, don't thank me! It's the very least I can smurf!
RRRRAM CLOBOP
BING
PWAAT
Article One! The Smurfs will respect and obey the Smurf King! All offenders will be severely smurfed!
Peyo
11

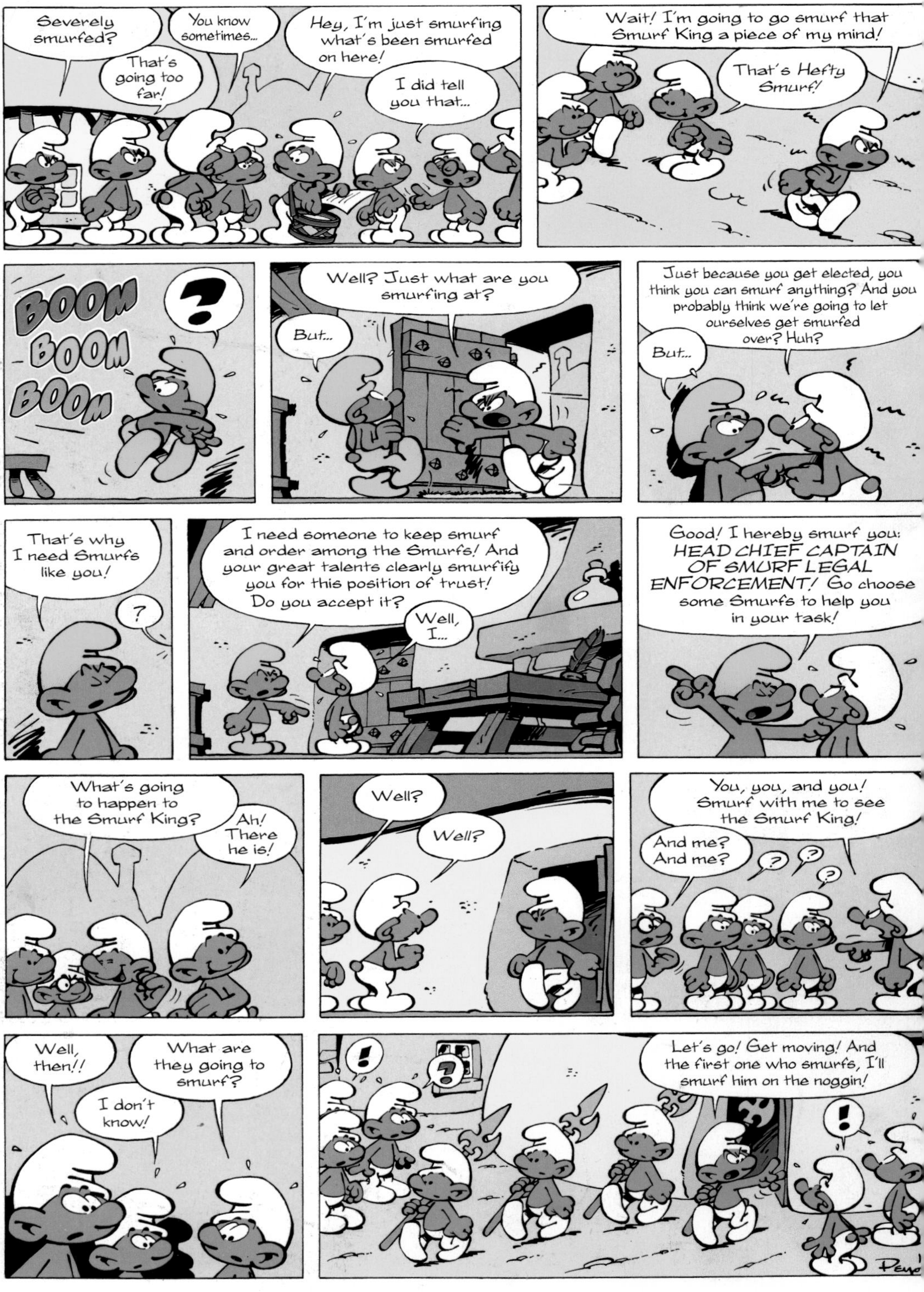

Severely smurfed?
That's going too far!
You know sometimes...
Hey, I'm just smurfing what's been smurfed on here!
I did tell you that...
Wait! I'm going to go smurf that Smurf King a piece of my mind!
That's Hefty Smurf!
BOOM BOOM BOOM
?
Well? Just what are you smurfing at?
But...
Just because you get elected, you think you can smurf anything? And you probably think we're going to let ourselves get smurfed over? Huh?
But...
That's why I need Smurfs like you!
?
I need someone to keep smurf and order among the Smurfs! And your great talents clearly smurfify you for this position of trust! Do you accept it?
Well, I...
Good! I hereby smurf you: HEAD CHIEF CAPTAIN OF SMURF LEGAL ENFORCEMENT! Go choose some Smurfs to help you in your task!
What's going to happen to the Smurf King?
Ah! There he is!
Well?
Well?
You, you, and you! Smurf with me to see the Smurf King!
And me? And me?
? ? ?
Well, then!!
What are they going to smurf?
I don't know!
!
?
Let's go! Get moving! And the first one who smurfs, I'll smurf him on the noggin!
!

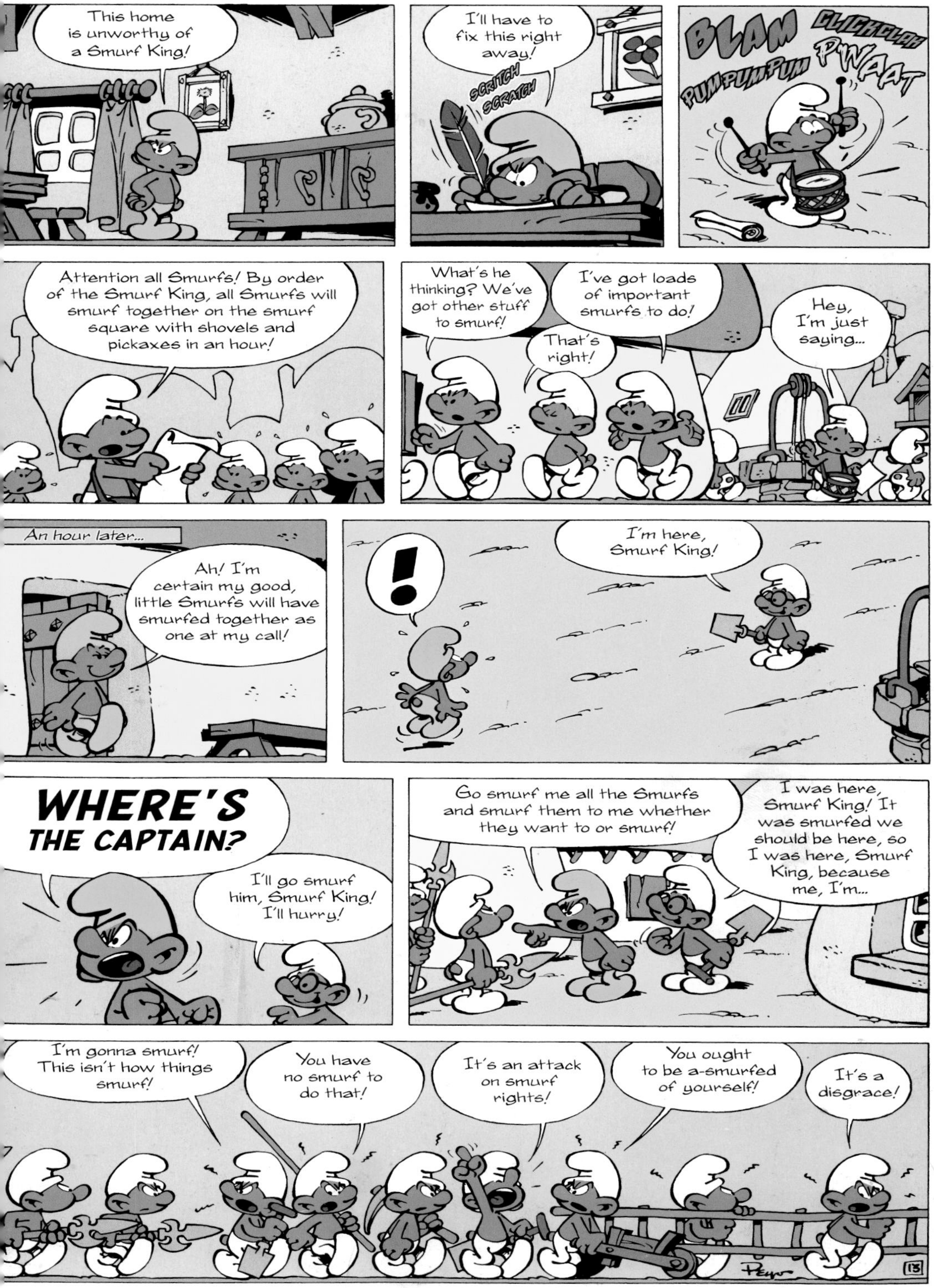

This home is unworthy of a Smurf King!
I'll have to fix this right away!
SCRITCH SCRATCH
BLAM CLICKCLACK PUMPUMPUM PWAAT
Attention all Smurfs! By order of the Smurf King, all Smurfs will smurf together on the smurf square with shovels and pickaxes in an hour!
What's he thinking? We've got other stuff to smurf!
I've got loads of important smurfs to do!
That's right!
Hey, I'm just saying...
An hour later...
Ah! I'm certain my good, little Smurfs will have smurfed together as one at my call!
!
I'm here, Smurf King!
WHERE'S THE CAPTAIN?
I'll go smurf him, Smurf King! I'll hurry!
Go smurf me all the Smurfs and smurf them to me whether they want to or smurf!
I was here, Smurf King! It was smurfed we should be here, so I was here, Smurf King, because me, I'm...
I'm gonna smurf! This isn't how things smurf!
You have no smurf to do that!
It's an attack on smurf rights!
You ought to be a-smurfed of yourself!
It's a disgrace!
13

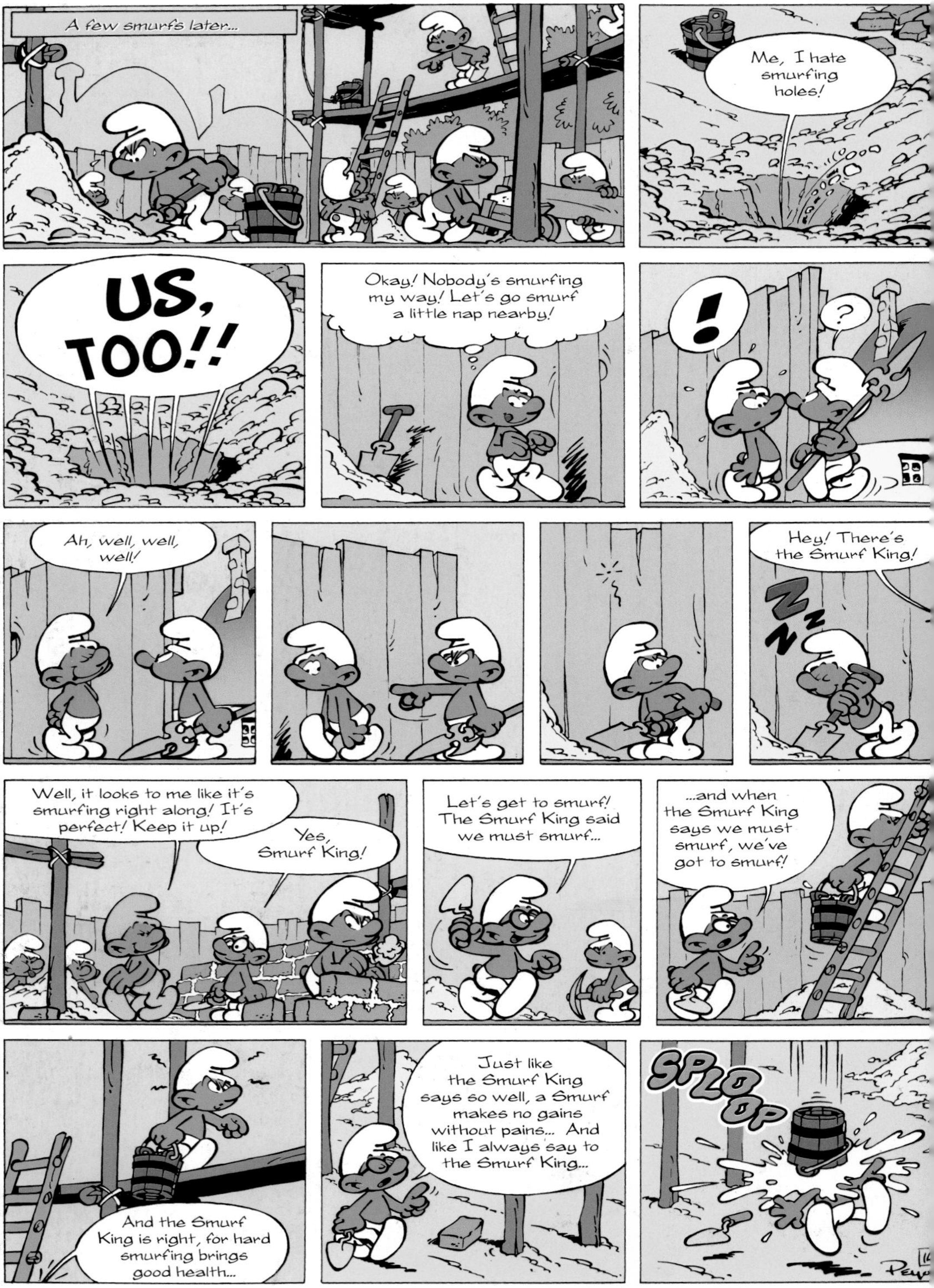
A few smurfs later...
Me, I hate smurfing holes!
US, TOO!!
Okay! Nobody's smurfing my way! Let's go smurf a little nap nearby!
!
?
Ah, well, well, well!
Hey! There's the Smurf King!
Well, it looks to me like it's smurfing right along! It's perfect! Keep it up!
Yes, Smurf King!
Let's get to smurf! The Smurf King said we must smurf...
...and when the Smurf King says we must smurf, we've got to smurf!
And the Smurf King is right, for hard smurfing brings good health...
Just like the Smurf King says so well, a Smurf makes no gains without pains... And like I always say to the Smurf King...
SPLOOP

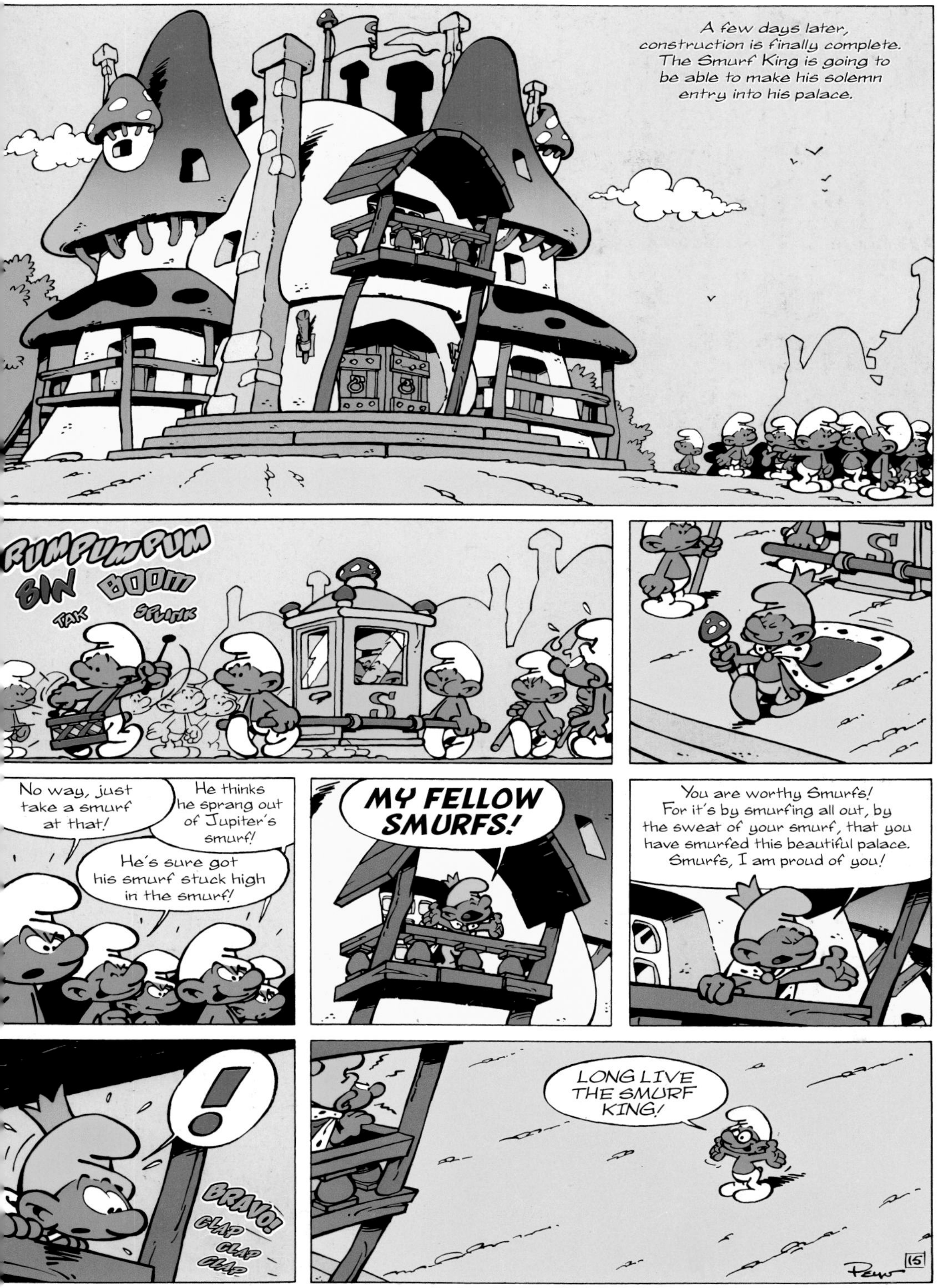

A few days later, construction is finally complete. The Smurf King is going to be able to make his solemn entry into his palace.
RUMPUMPUM
BIN
BOOM
TAK
SPLINK
No way, just take a smurf at that!
He thinks he sprang out of Jupiter's smurf!
He's sure got his smurf stuck high in the smurf!
MY FELLOW SMURFS!
You are worthy Smurfs! For it's by smurfing all out, by the sweat of your smurf, that you have smurfed this beautiful palace. Smurfs, I am proud of you!
!
BRAVO!
CLAP
CLAP
CLAP
LONG LIVE THE SMURF KING!
15

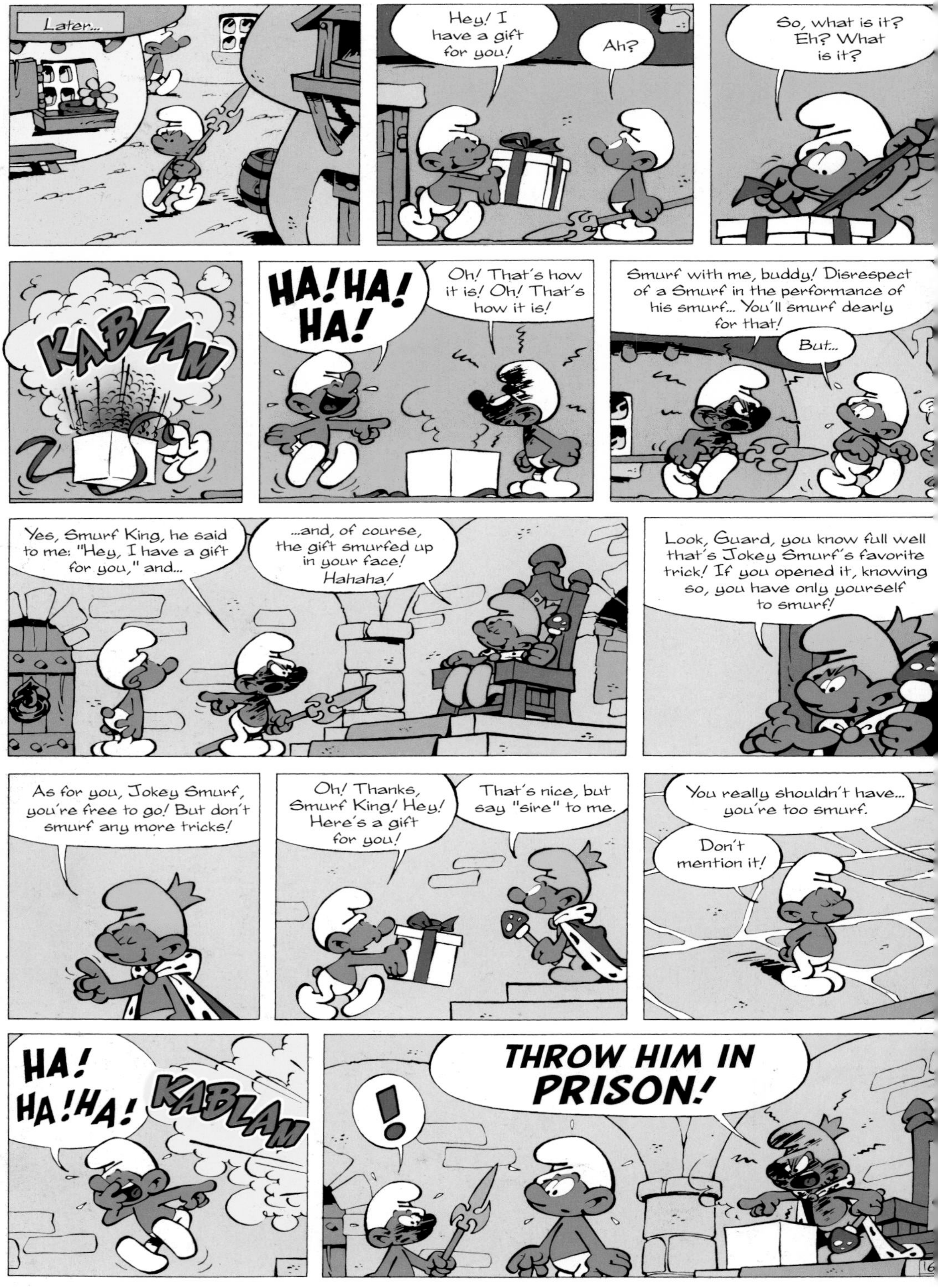

Later...
Hey! I have a gift for you!
Ah?
So, what is it? Eh? What is it?
KABLAM
HA!HA! HA!
Oh! That's how it is! Oh! That's how it is!
Smurf with me, buddy! Disrespect of a Smurf in the performance of his smurf... You'll smurf dearly for that!
But...
Yes, Smurf King, he said to me: "Hey, I have a gift for you," and...
...and, of course, the gift smurfed up in your face! Hahaha!
Look, Guard, you know full well that's Jokey Smurf's favorite trick! If you opened it, knowing so, you have only yourself to smurf!
As for you, Jokey Smurf, you're free to go! But don't smurf any more tricks!
Oh! Thanks, Smurf King! Hey! Here's a gift for you!
That's nice, but say "sire" to me.
You really shouldn't have... you're too smurf.
Don't mention it!
HA! HA!HA!
KABLAM
!
THROW HIM IN PRISON!
16

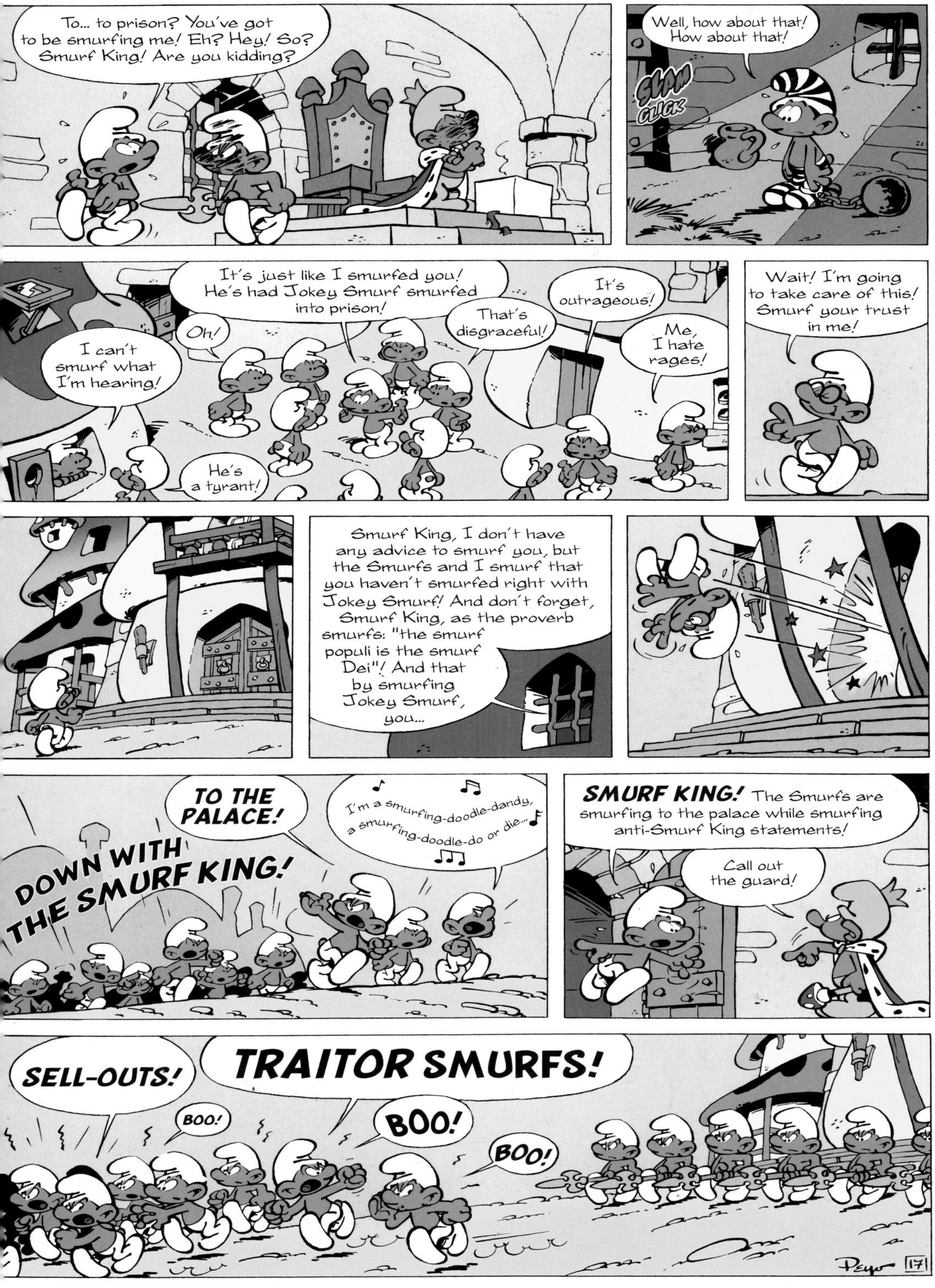
To... to prison? You've got to be smurfing me! Eh? Hey! So? Smurf King! Are you kidding?
Well, how about that! How about that!
SLAM
CLICK
It's just like I smurfed you! He's had Jokey Smurf smurfed into prison!
I can't smurf what I'm hearing!
Oh!
That's disgraceful!
It's outrageous!
Me, I hate rages!
He's a tyrant!
Wait! I'm going to take care of this! Smurf your trust in me!
Smurf King, I don't have any advice to smurf you, but the Smurfs and I smurf that you haven't smurfed right with Jokey Smurf! And don't forget, Smurf King, as the proverb smurfs: "the smurf populi is the smurf Dei"! And that by smurfing Jokey Smurf, you...
TO THE PALACE!
DOWN WITH THE SMURF KING!
I'm a smurfing-doodle-dandy, a smurfing-doodle-do or die...
SMURF KING! The Smurfs are smurfing to the palace while smurfing anti-Smurf King statements!
Call out the guard!
SELL-OUTS!
TRAITOR SMURFS!
BOO!
BOO!
BOO!
Peyo
17

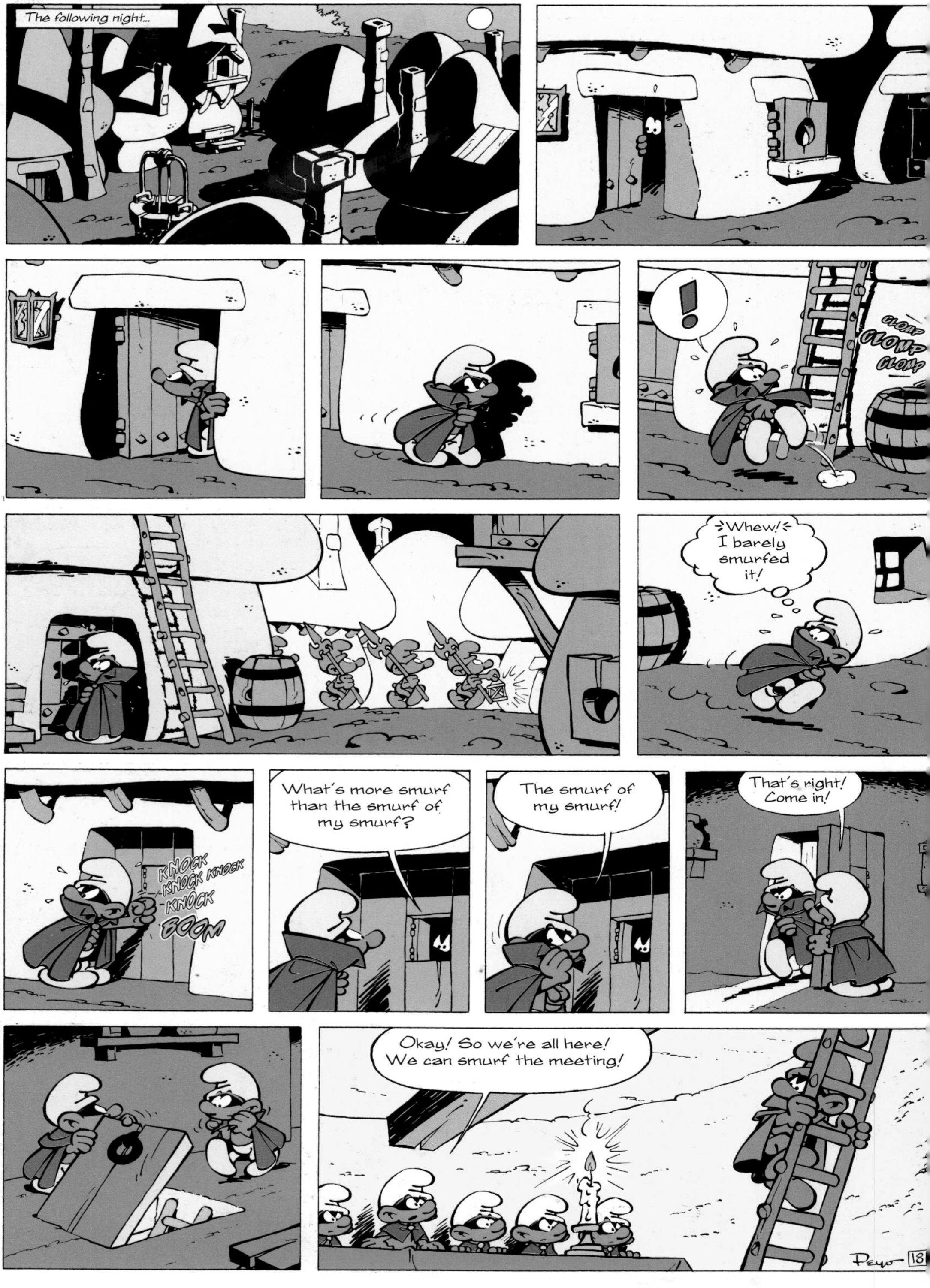
The following night...
!
CLOMP CLOMP CLOMP
Whew! I barely smurfed it!
KNOCK KNOCK KNOCK KNOCK
BOOM
What's more smurf than the smurf of my smurf?
The smurf of my smurf!
That's right! Come in!
Okay! So we're all here! We can smurf the meeting!
Peyo 18

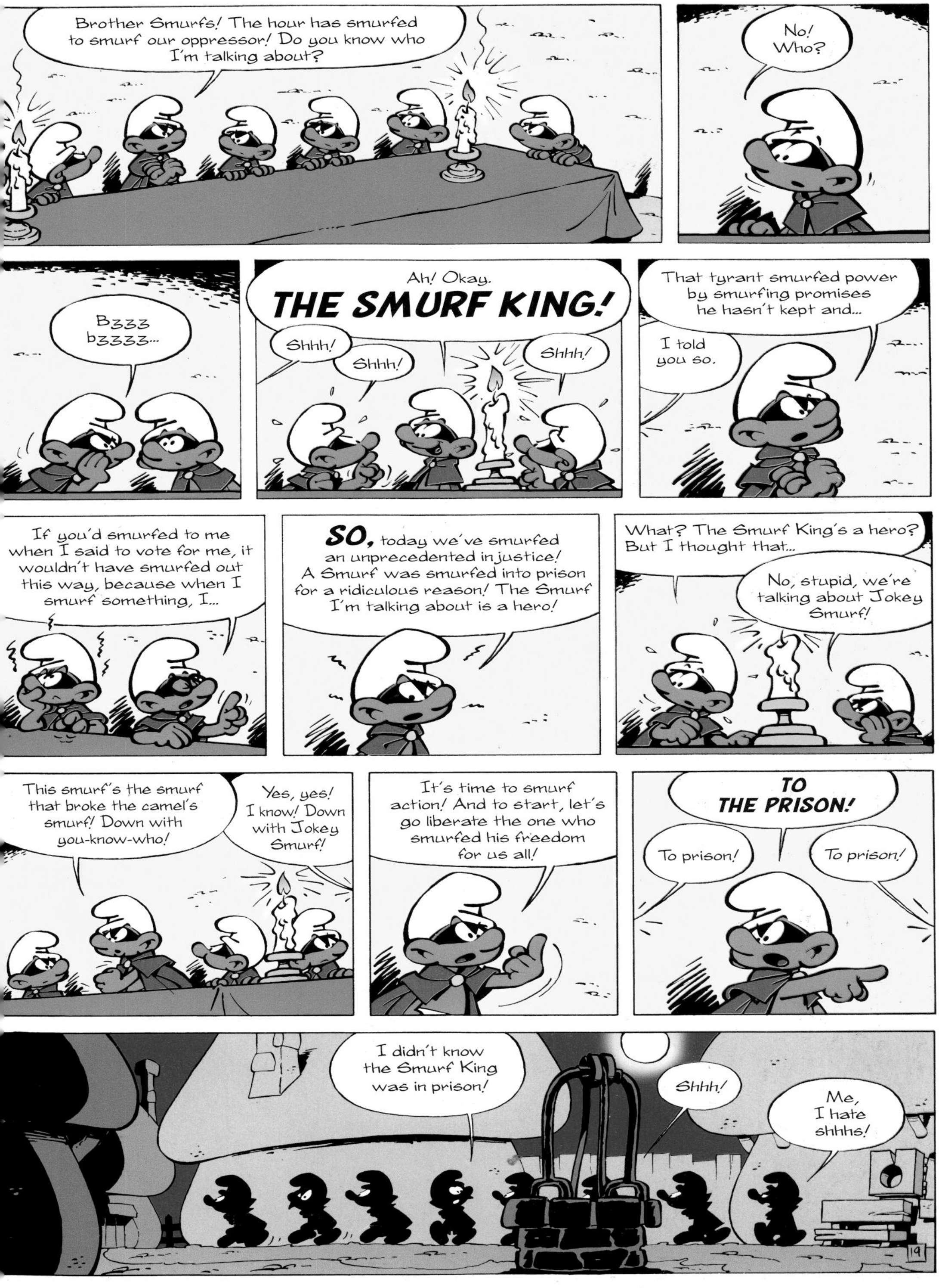
Brother Smurfs! The hour has smurfed to smurf our oppressor! Do you know who I'm talking about?
No! Who?
Bzzz bzzzz...
Ah! Okay. THE SMURF KING!
Shhh!
Shhh!
Shhh!
That tyrant smurfed power by smurfing promises he hasn't kept and...
I told you so.
If you'd smurfed to me when I said to vote for me, it wouldn't have smurfed out this way, because when I smurf something, I...
SO, today we've smurfed an unprecedented injustice! A Smurf was smurfed into prison for a ridiculous reason! The Smurf I'm talking about is a hero!
What? The Smurf King's a hero? But I thought that...
No, stupid, we're talking about Jokey Smurf!
This smurf's the smurf that broke the camel's smurf! Down with you-know-who!
Yes, yes! I know! Down with Jokey Smurf!
It's time to smurf action! And to start, let's go liberate the one who smurfed his freedom for us all!
TO THE PRISON!
To prison!
To prison!
I didn't know the Smurf King was in prison!
Shhh!
Me, I hate shhhs!
19

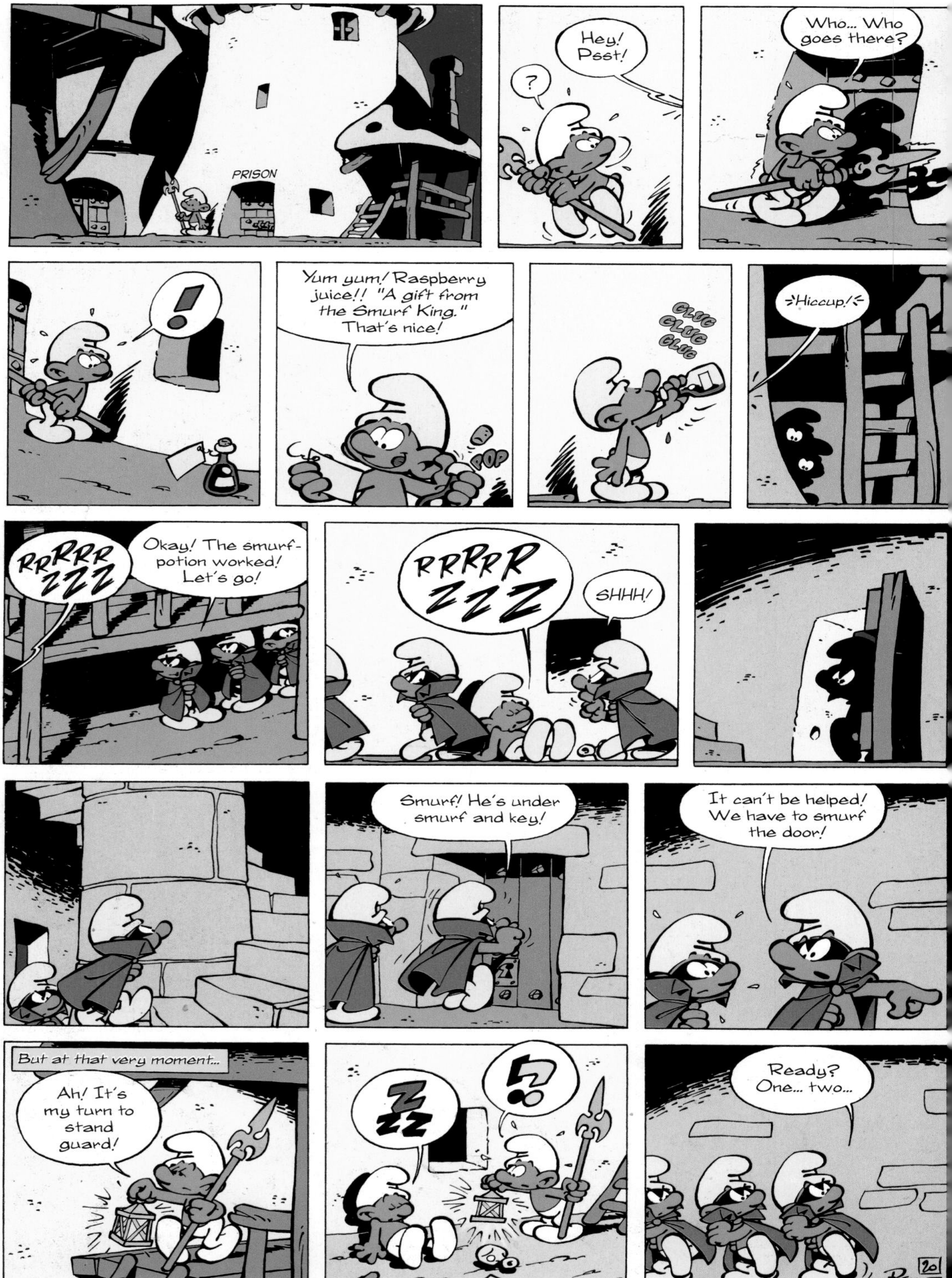
PRISON
Hey! Psst!
?
Who... Who goes there?
!
Yum yum! Raspberry juice!! "A gift from the Smurf King." That's nice!
POP
GLUG GLUG GLUG
Hiccup!
RRRRR ZZZ
Okay! The smurf-potion worked! Let's go!
RRRRR ZZZ
SHHH!
Smurf! He's under smurf and key!
It can't be helped! We have to smurf the door!
But at that very moment...
Ah! It's my turn to stand guard!
ZZZ
?
Ready? One... two...
20
Peyo

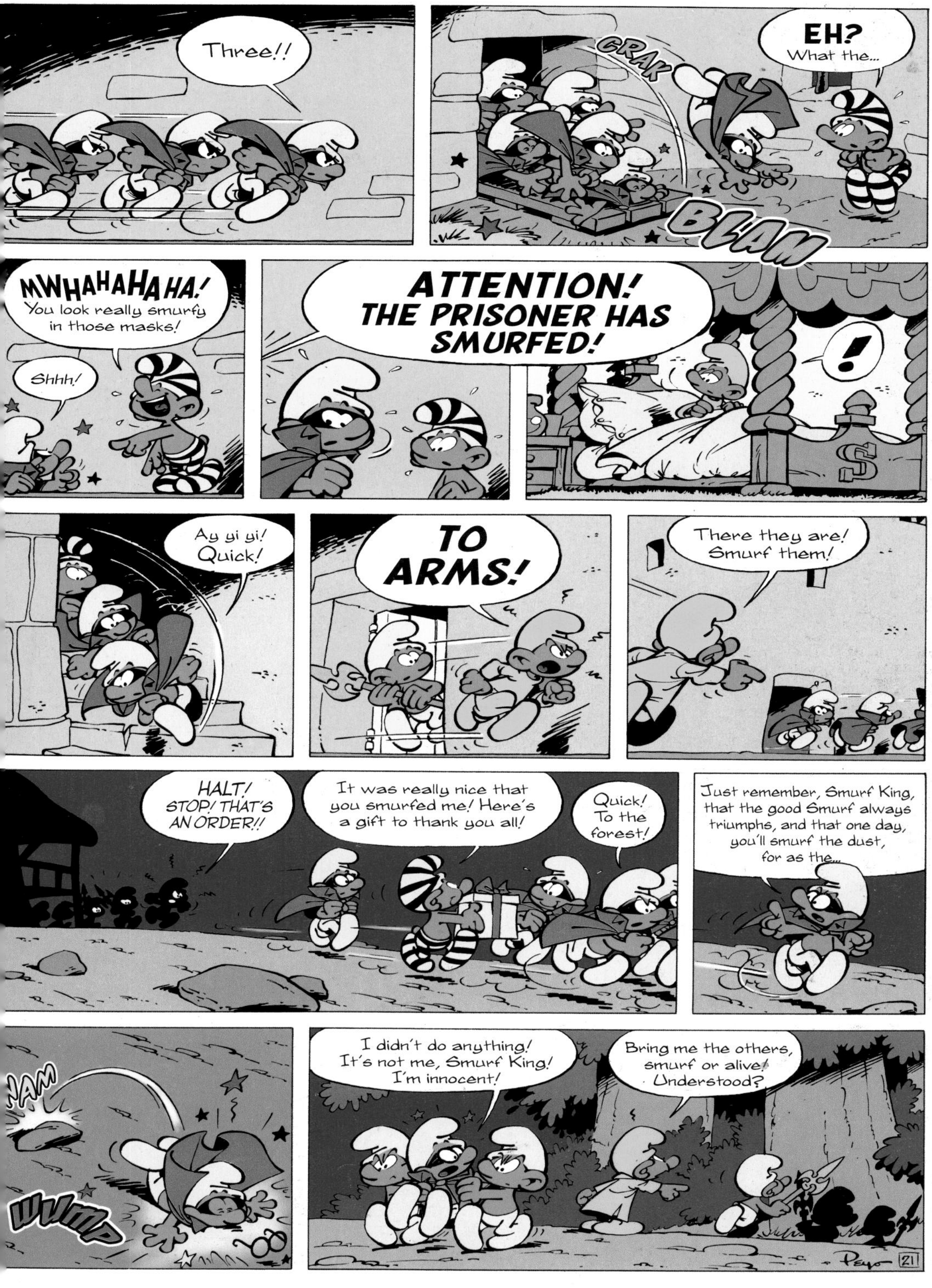

Three!!
CRAK
EH?
What the...
BLAM
MWHAHAHAHA!
You look really smurfy in those masks!
Shhh!
ATTENTION!
THE PRISONER HAS SMURFED!
!
Ay yi yi!
Quick!
TO ARMS!
There they are!
Smurf them!
HALT!
STOP! THAT'S AN ORDER!!
It was really nice that you smurfed me! Here's a gift to thank you all!
Quick!
To the forest!
Just remember, Smurf King, that the good Smurf always triumphs, and that one day, you'll smurf the dust, for as the...
WHAM
WUMP
I didn't do anything!
It's not me, Smurf King!
I'm innocent!
Bring me the others, smurf or alive!
Understood?
Peyo
21

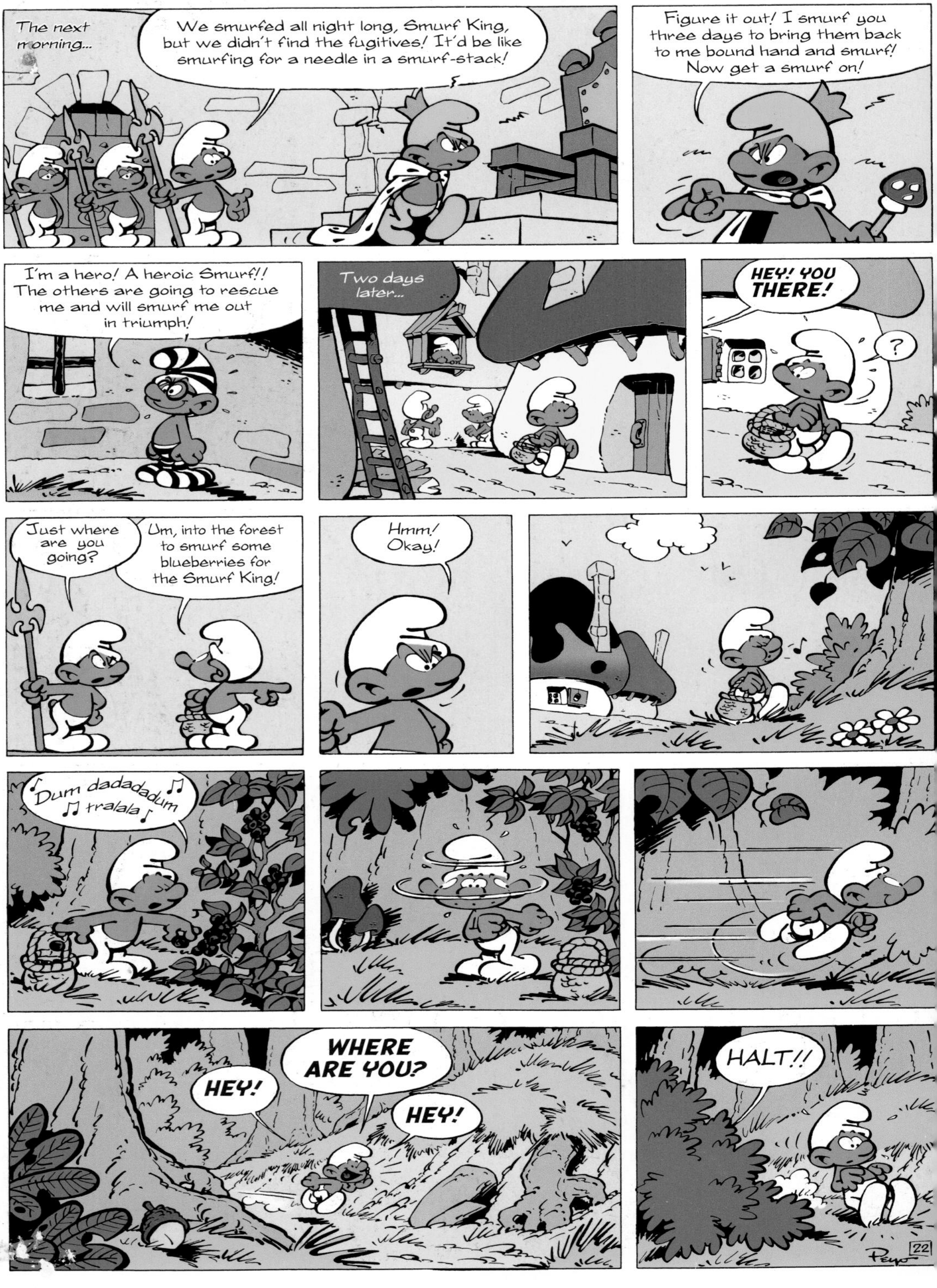

The next morning...
We smurfed all night long, Smurf King, but we didn't find the fugitives! It'd be like smurfing for a needle in a smurf-stack!
Figure it out! I smurf you three days to bring them back to me bound hand and smurf! Now get a smurf on!
I'm a hero! A heroic Smurf!! The others are going to rescue me and will smurf me out in triumph!
Two days later...
HEY! YOU THERE!
?
Just where are you going?
Um, into the forest to smurf some blueberries for the Smurf King!
Hmm! Okay!
Dum dadadadum tralala
WHERE ARE YOU?
HEY!
HEY!
HALT!!
Peyo
22

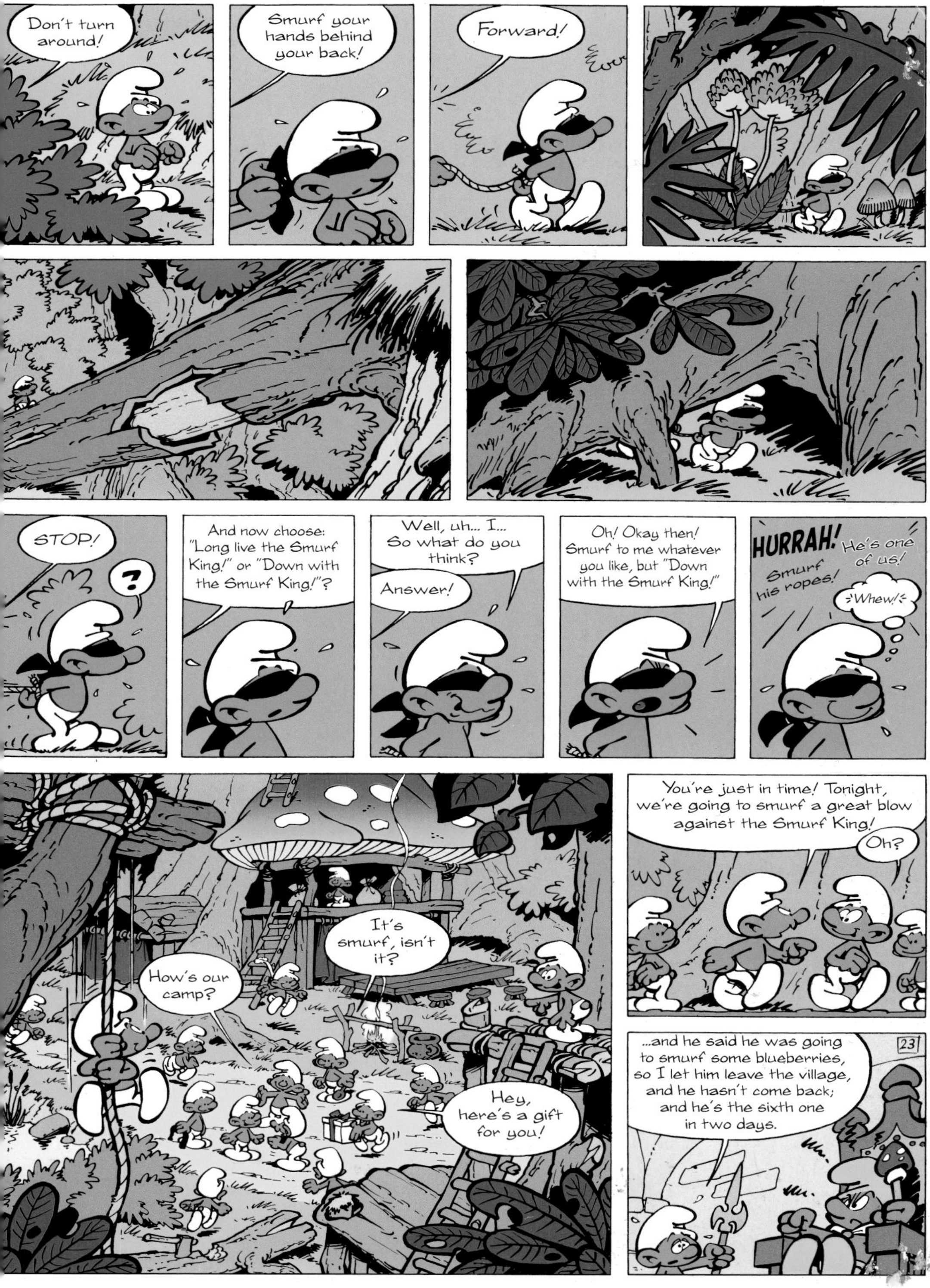
Don't turn around!
Smurf your hands behind your back!
Forward!
STOP!
?
And now choose: "Long live the Smurf King!" or "Down with the Smurf King!"?
Well, uh... I... So what do you think?
Answer!
Oh! Okay then! Smurf to me whatever you like, but "Down with the Smurf King!"
HURRAH!
He's one of us!
Smurf his ropes!
Whew!
How's our camp?
It's smurf, isn't it?
Hey, here's a gift for you!
You're just in time! Tonight, we're going to smurf a great blow against the Smurf King!
Oh?
23
...and he said he was going to smurf some blueberries, so I let him leave the village, and he hasn't come back; and he's the sixth one in two days.

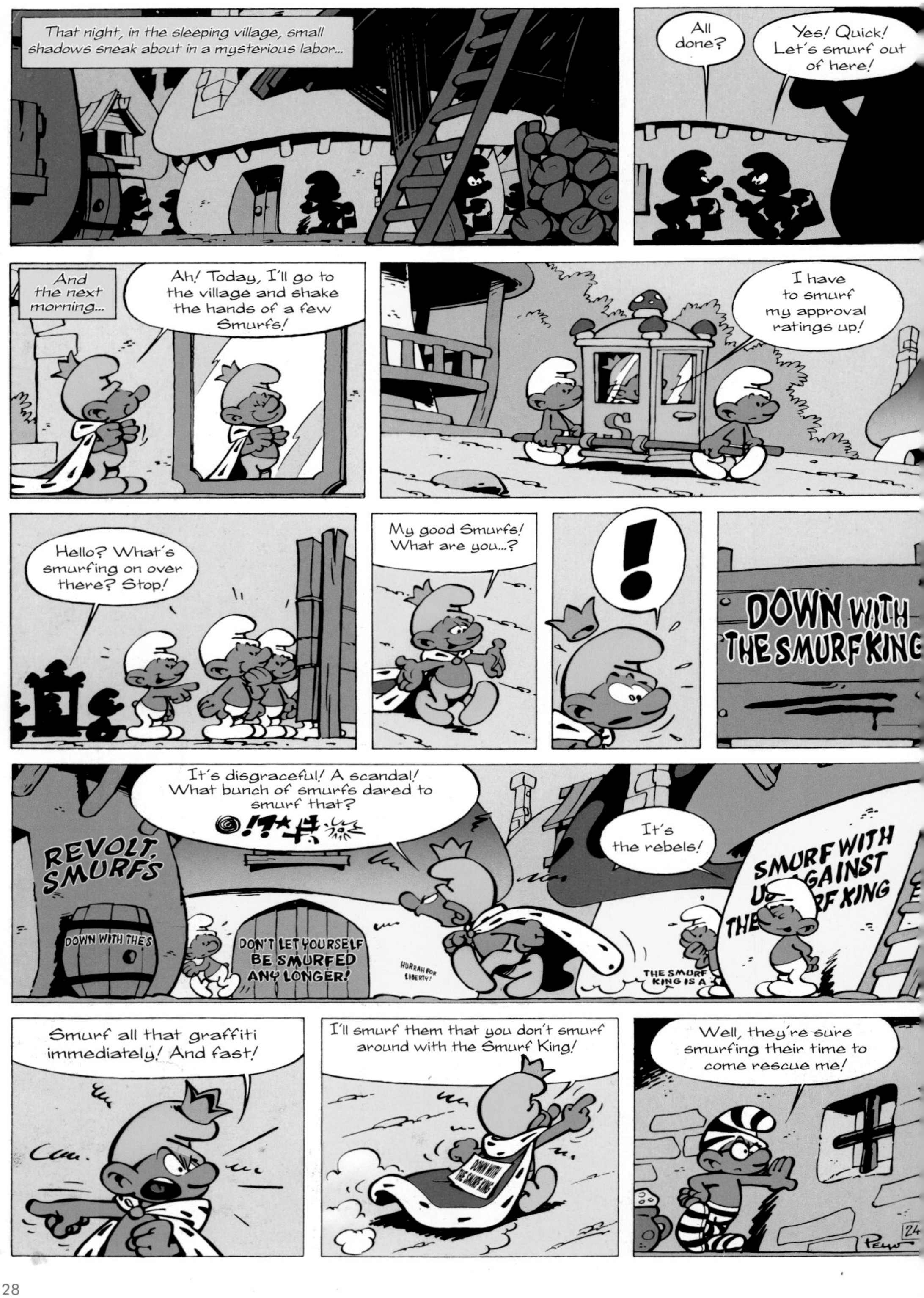

That night, in the sleeping village, small shadows sneak about in a mysterious labor...
All done?
Yes! Quick! Let's smurf out of here!
And the next morning...
Ah! Today, I'll go to the village and shake the hands of a few Smurfs!
I have to smurf my approval ratings up!
Hello? What's smurfing on over there? Stop!
My good Smurfs! What are you...?
!
DOWN WITH THE SMURF KING
It's disgraceful! A scandal! What bunch of smurfs dared to smurf that?
It's the rebels!
REVOLT, SMURFS
DOWN WITH THE S
DON'T LET YOURSELF BE SMURFED ANY LONGER!
HURRAH FOR LIBERTY!
THE SMURF KING IS A
SMURF WITH U AGAINST THE RF KING
Smurf all that graffiti immediately! And fast!
I'll smurf them that you don't smurf around with the Smurf King!
DOWN WITH THE SMURF KING
Well, they're sure smurfing their time to come rescue me!

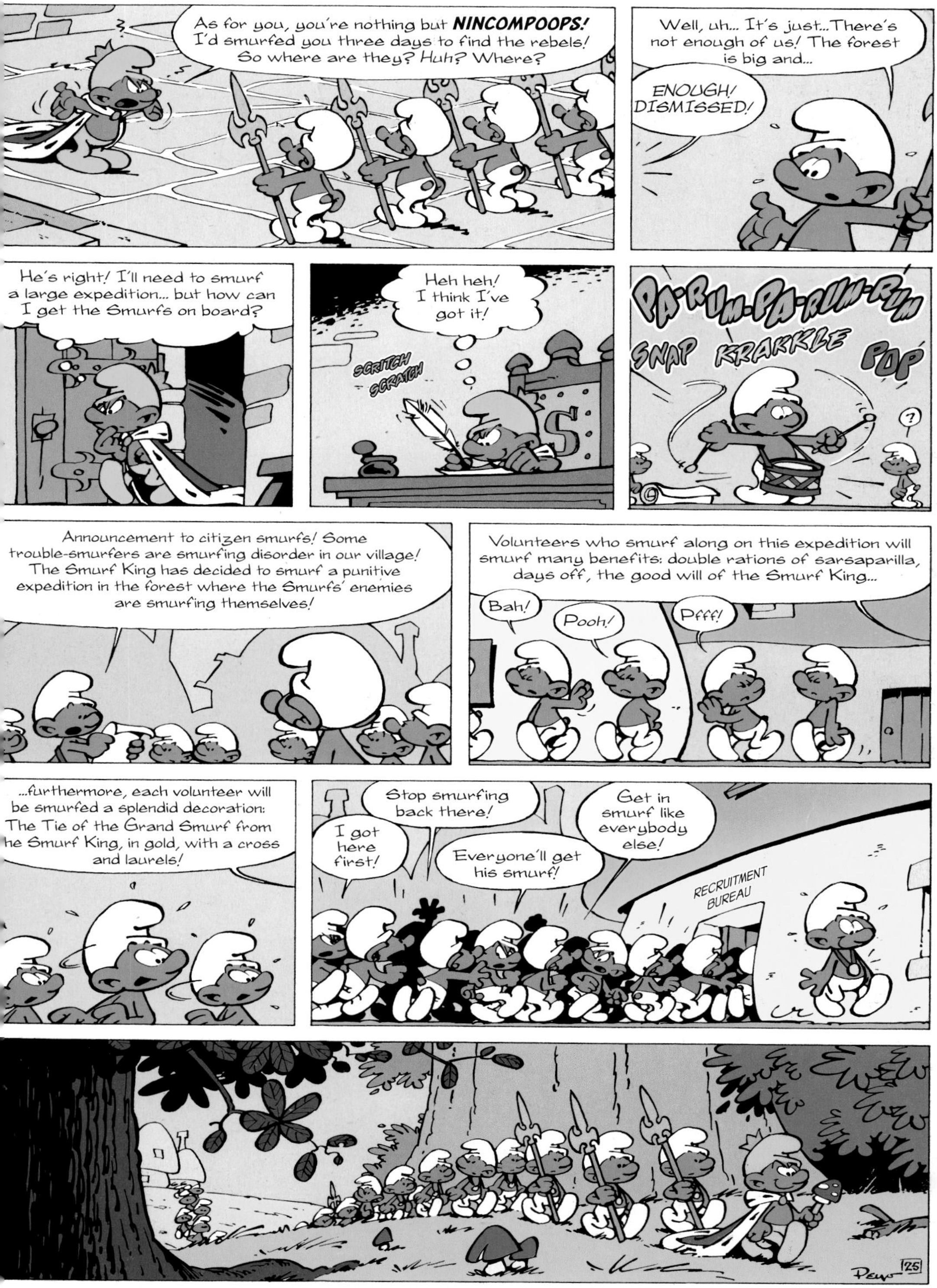
As for you, you're nothing but NINCOMPOOPS! I'd smurfed you three days to find the rebels! So where are they? Huh? Where?
Well, uh... It's just...There's not enough of us! The forest is big and...
ENOUGH! DISMISSED!
He's right! I'll need to smurf a large expedition... but how can I get the Smurfs on board?
Heh heh! I think I've got it!
SCRITCH SCRATCH
PA-RUM-PA-RUM-RUM
SNAP KRAKKLE POP
Announcement to citizen smurfs! Some trouble-smurfers are smurfing disorder in our village! The Smurf King has decided to smurf a punitive expedition in the forest where the Smurfs' enemies are smurfing themselves!
Volunteers who smurf along on this expedition will smurf many benefits: double rations of sarsaparilla, days off, the good will of the Smurf King...
Bah!
Pooh!
Pfff!
...furthermore, each volunteer will be smurfed a splendid decoration: The Tie of the Grand Smurf from he Smurf King, in gold, with a cross and laurels!
I got here first!
Stop smurfing back there!
Everyone'll get his smurf!
Get in smurf like everybody else!
RECRUITMENT BUREAU
25

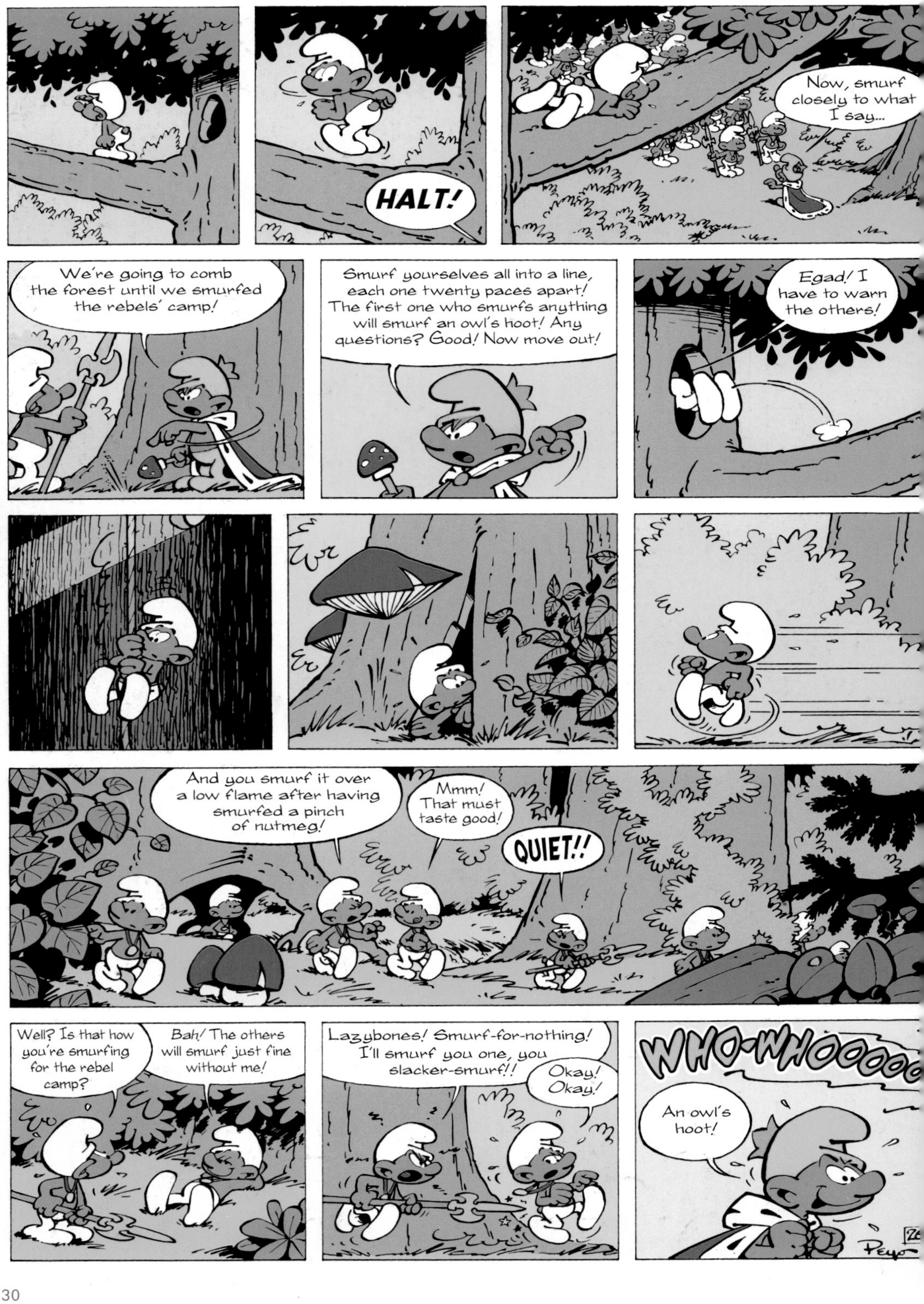
HALT!
Now, smurf closely to what I say...
We're going to comb the forest until we smurfed the rebels' camp!
Smurf yourselves all into a line, each one twenty paces apart! The first one who smurfs anything will smurf an owl's hoot! Any questions? Good! Now move out!
Egad! I have to warn the others!
And you smurf it over a low flame after having smurfed a pinch of nutmeg!
Mmm! That must taste good!
QUIET!!
Well? Is that how you're smurfing for the rebel camp?
Bah! The others will smurf just fine without me!
Lazybones! Smurf-for-nothing! I'll smurf you one, you slacker-smurf!!
Okay! Okay!
WHO-WHOOOOO
An owl's hoot!

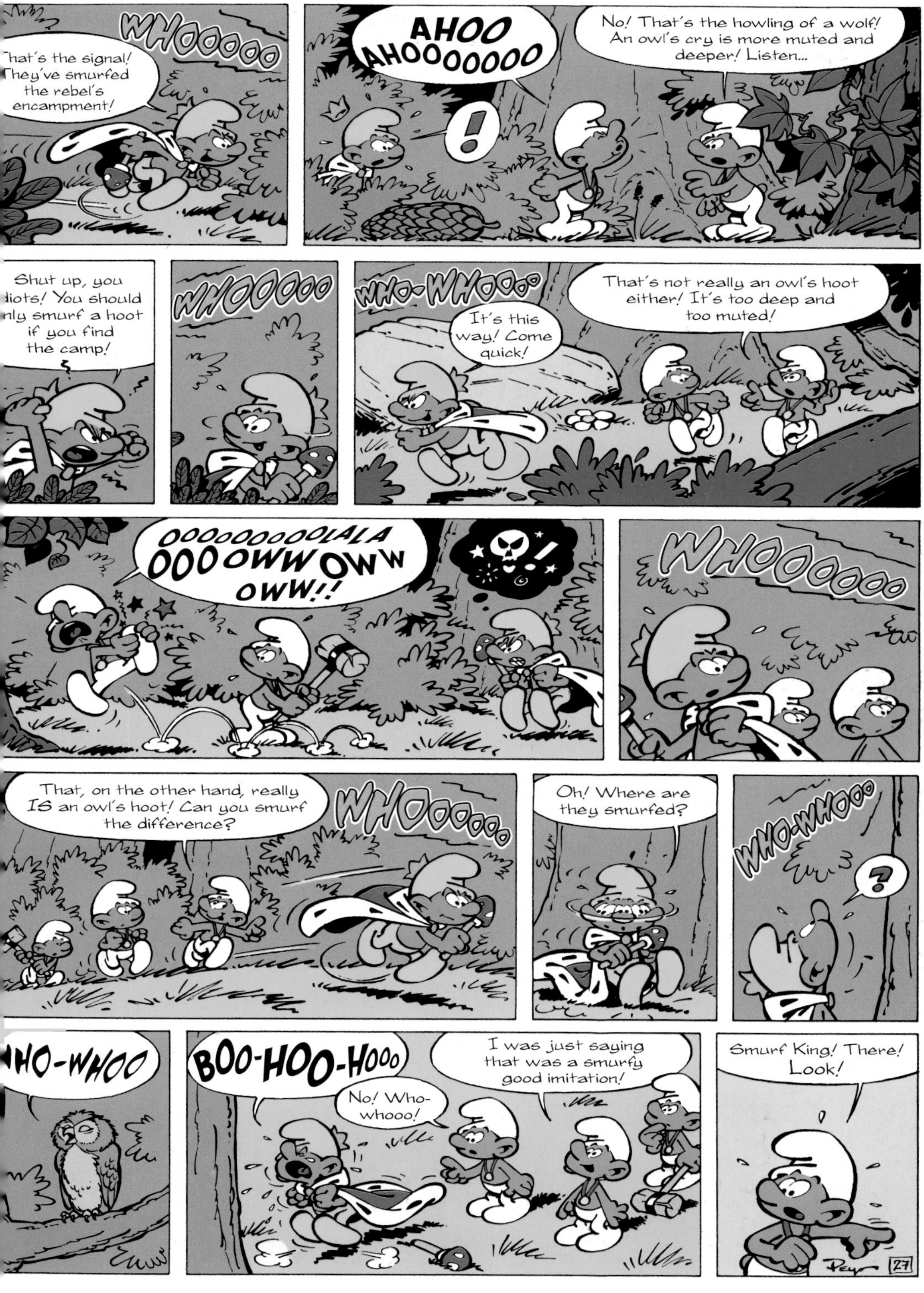

WHOOOOOO
That's the signal! They've smurfed the rebel's encampment!
AHOO AHOOOOOOO
!
No! That's the howling of a wolf! An owl's cry is more muted and deeper! Listen...
Shut up, you idiots! You should only smurf a hoot if you find the camp!
WHOOOOOO
WHO-WHOOOO
It's this way! Come quick!
That's not really an owl's hoot either! It's too deep and too muted!
OOOOOOOOOLALA OOO OWW OWW OWW!!
WHOOOOOOO
That, on the other hand, really IS an owl's hoot! Can you smurf the difference?
WHOOOOOOO
Oh! Where are they smurfed?
WHO-WHOOO
?
WHO-WHOO
BOO-HOO-HOOO
No! Who-whooo!
I was just saying that was a smurfy good imitation!
Smurf King! There! Look!
Peyo
27

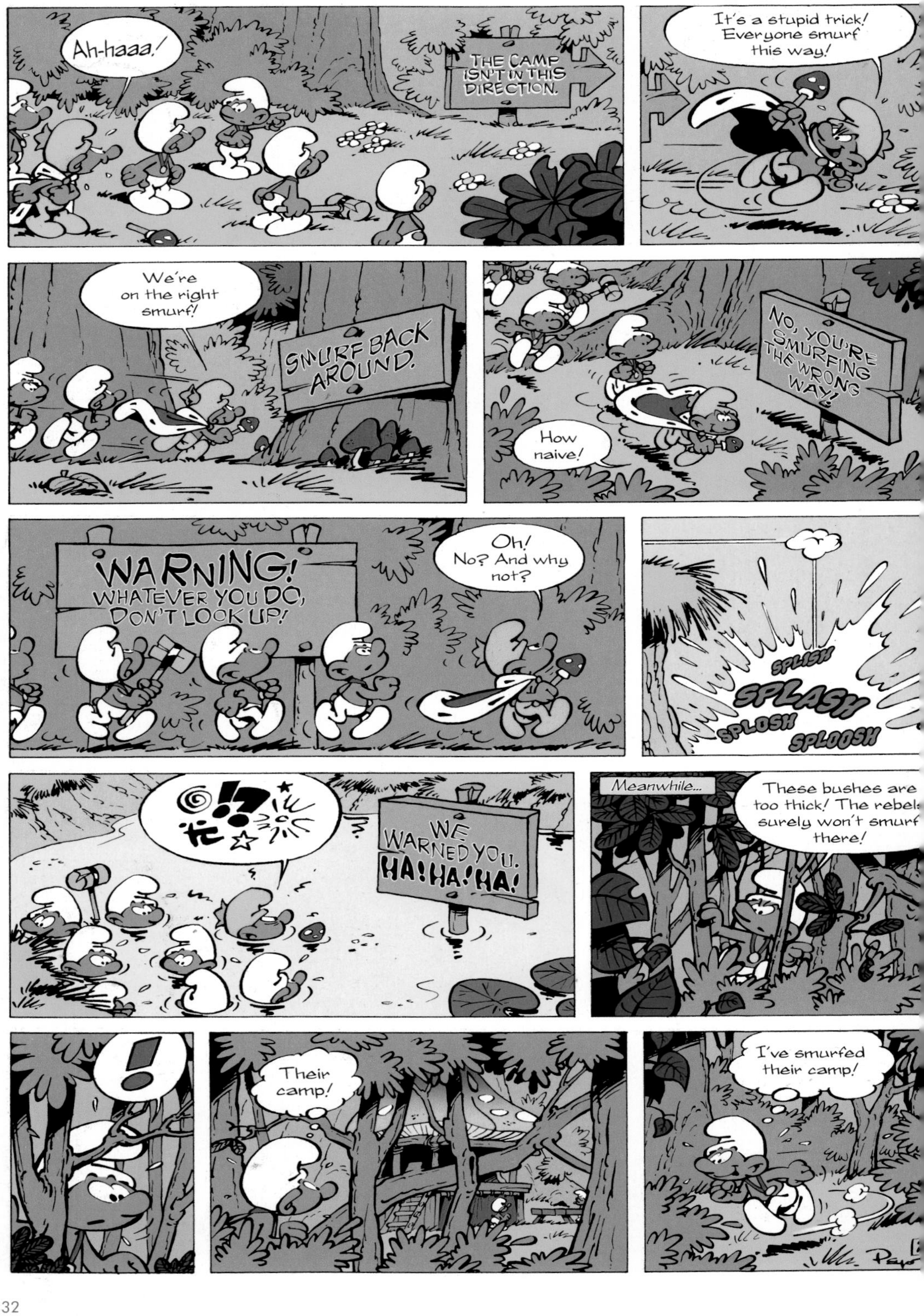

Ah-haaa!
THE CAMP ISN'T IN THIS DIRECTION.
It's a stupid trick! Everyone smurf this way!
We're on the right smurf!
SMURF BACK AROUND.
NO, YOU'RE SMURFING THE WRONG WAY!
How naive!
WARNING! WHATEVER YOU DO, DON'T LOOK UP!
Oh! No? And why not?
SPLISH
SPLASH
SPLOSH
SPLOOSH
WE WARNED YOU. HA! HA! HA!
Meanwhile...
These bushes are too thick! The rebels surely won't smurf there!
!
Their camp!
I've smurfed their camp!

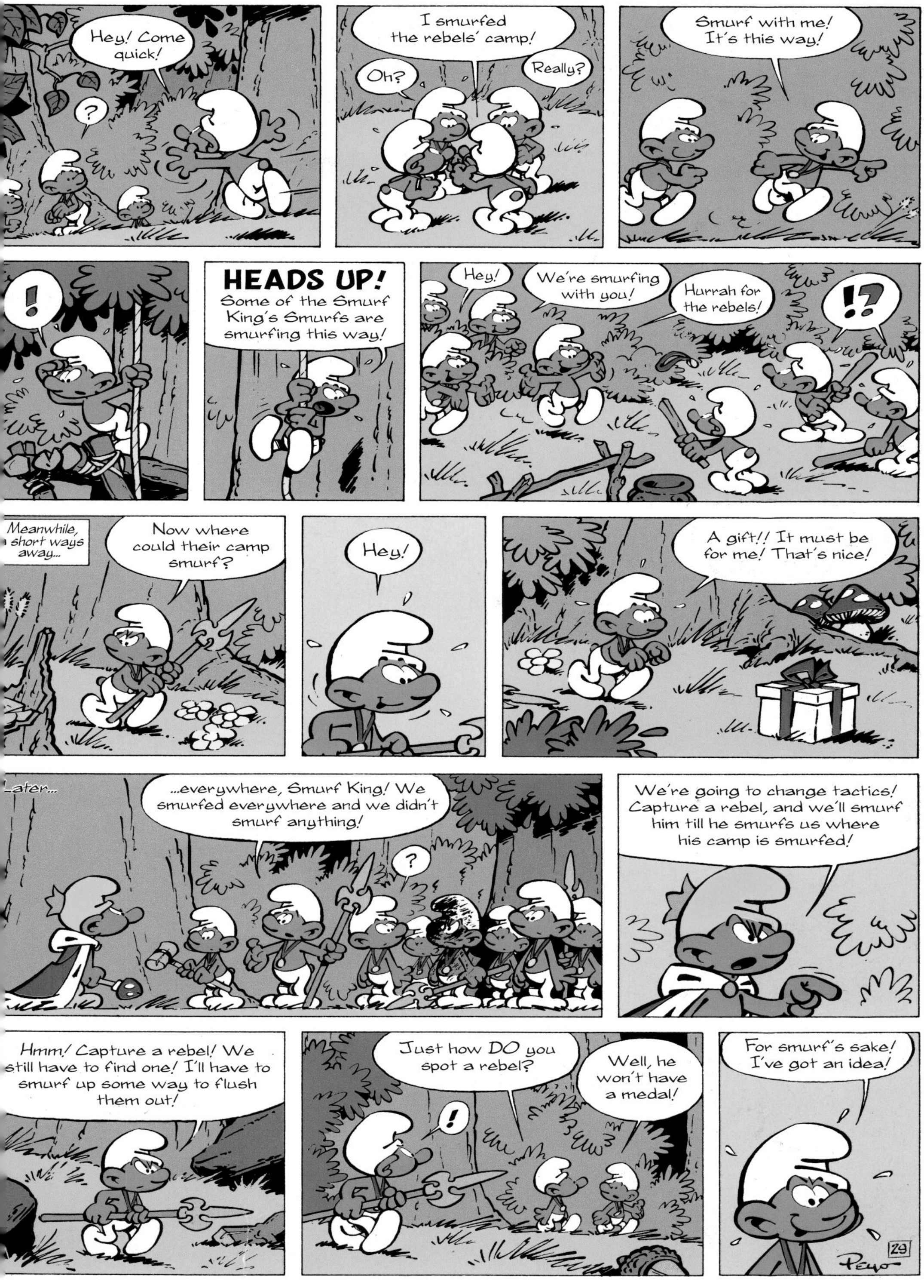

Hey! Come quick!
?
I smurfed the rebels' camp!
Oh?
Really?
Smurf with me! It's this way!
!
HEADS UP! Some of the Smurf King's Smurfs are smurfing this way!
Hey!
We're smurfing with you!
Hurrah for the rebels!
!?
Meanwhile, a short ways away...
Now where could their camp smurf?
Hey!
A gift!! It must be for me! That's nice!
Later...
...everywhere, Smurf King! We smurfed everywhere and we didn't smurf anything!
?
We're going to change tactics! Capture a rebel, and we'll smurf him till he smurfs us where his camp is smurfed!
Hmm! Capture a rebel! We still have to find one! I'll have to smurf up some way to flush them out!
Just how DO you spot a rebel?
Well, he won't have a medal!
!
For smurf's sake! I've got an idea!
29
Peyo

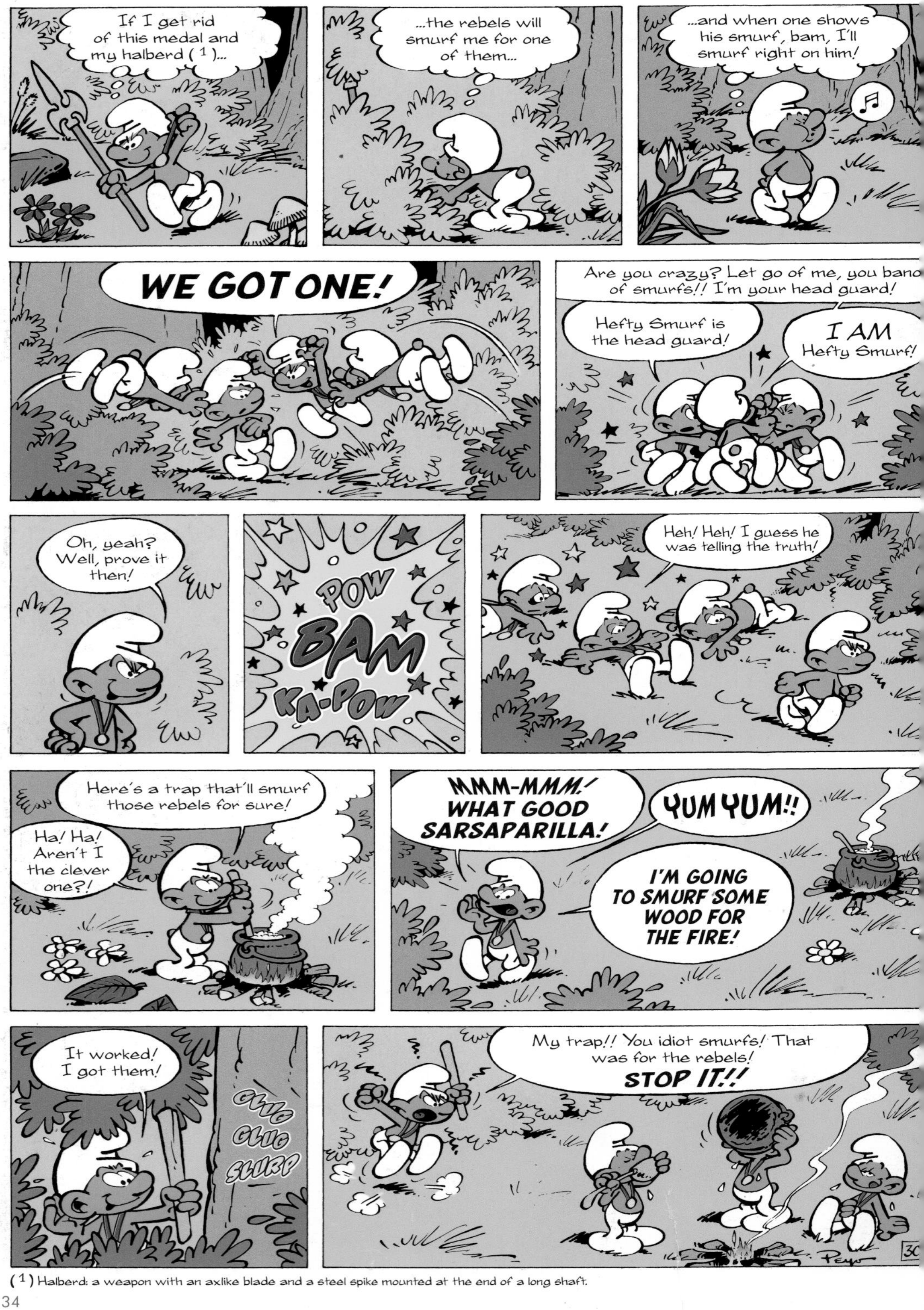
If I get rid of this medal and my halberd (1)...
...the rebels will smurf me for one of them...
...and when one shows his smurf, bam, I'll smurf right on him!
WE GOT ONE!
Are you crazy? Let go of me, you band of smurfs!! I'm your head guard!
Hefty Smurf is the head guard!
I AM Hefty Smurf!
Oh, yeah? Well, prove it then!
POW
BAM
KA-POW
Heh! Heh! I guess he was telling the truth!
Here's a trap that'll smurf those rebels for sure!
Ha! Ha! Aren't I the clever one?!
MMM-MMM! WHAT GOOD SARSAPARILLA!
YUM YUM!!
I'M GOING TO SMURF SOME WOOD FOR THE FIRE!
It worked! I got them!
GLUG GLUG SLURP
My trap!! You idiot smurfs! That was for the rebels! STOP IT!!

(1) Halberd: a weapon with an axlike blade and a steel spike mounted at the end of a long shaft.

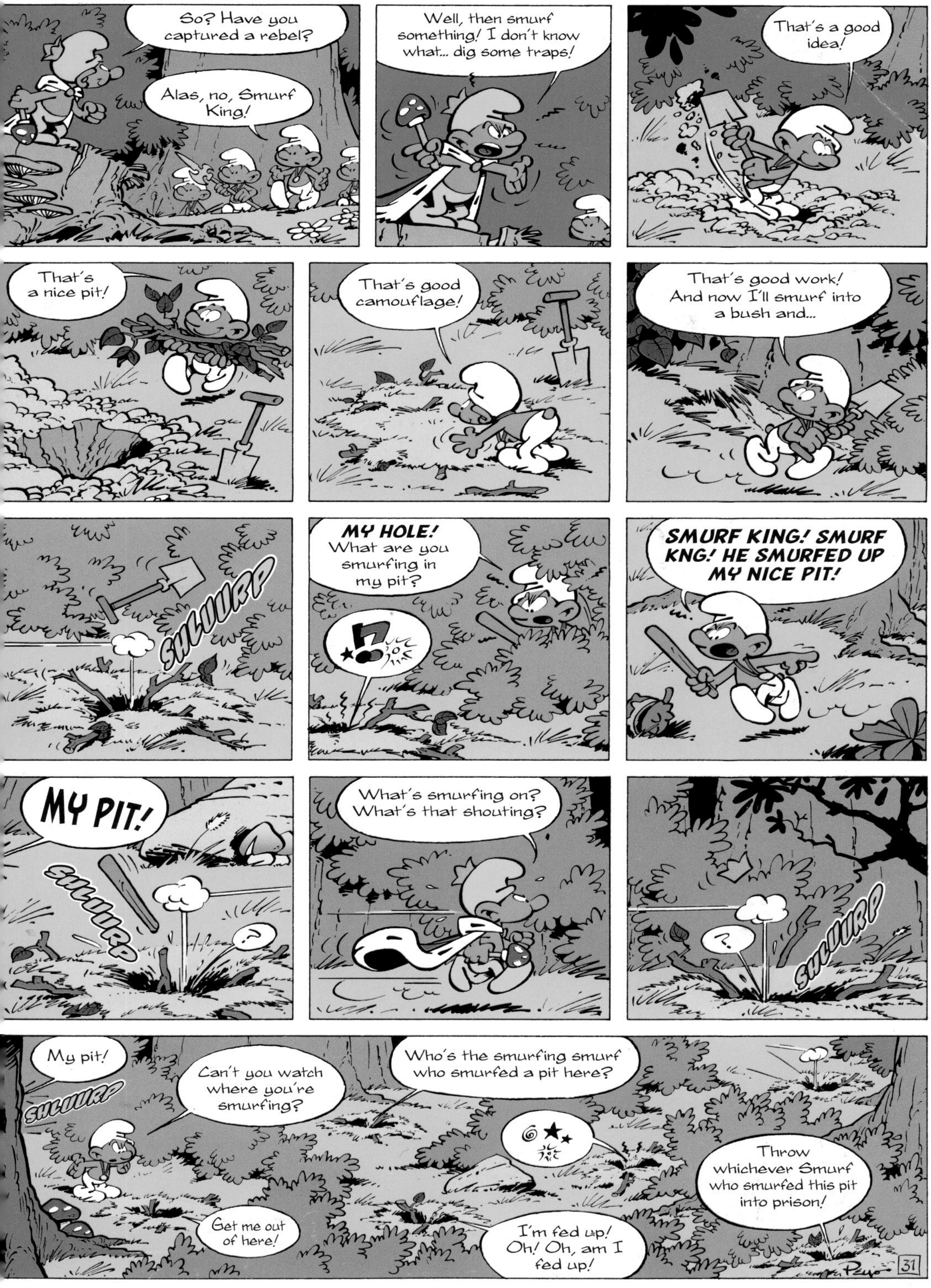
So? Have you captured a rebel?
Alas, no, Smurf King!
Well, then smurf something! I don't know what... dig some traps!
That's a good idea!
That's a nice pit!
That's good camouflage!
That's good work! And now I'll smurf into a bush and...
SHLUURP
MY HOLE! What are you smurfing in my pit?
SMURF KING! SMURF KNG! HE SMURFED UP MY NICE PIT!
MY PIT!
SHLUURP
What's smurfing on? What's that shouting?
SHLUURP
My pit!
SHLUURP
Can't you watch where you're smurfing?
Who's the smurfing smurf who smurfed a pit here?
Throw whichever Smurf who smurfed this pit into prison!
Get me out of here!
I'm fed up! Oh! Oh, am I fed up!
31

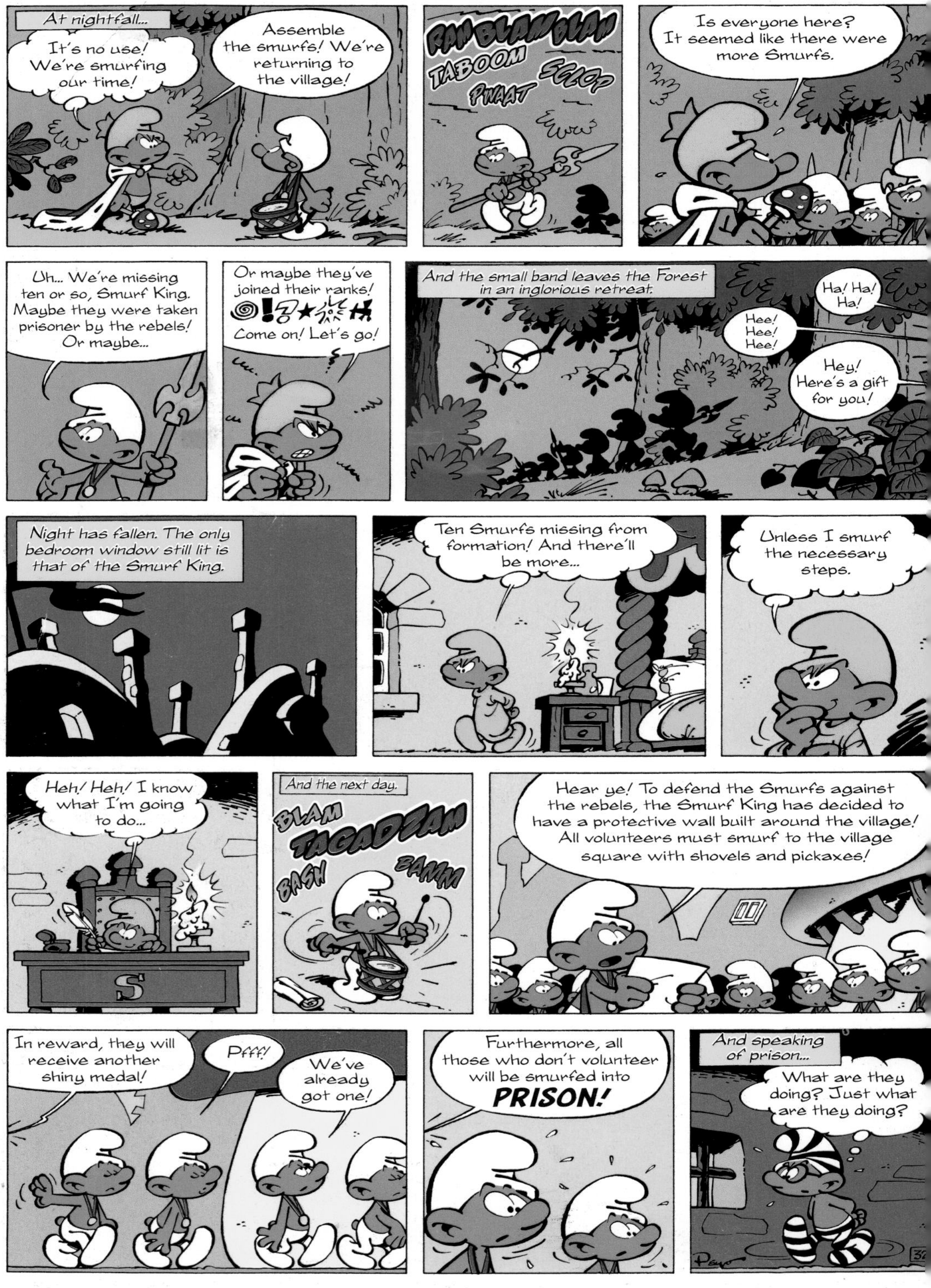

At nightfall...
It's no use! We're smurfing our time!
Assemble the smurfs! We're returning to the village!
RAN BLAM BLAM
TABOOM
SCLOP
PWAAT
Is everyone here? It seemed like there were more Smurfs.
Uh... We're missing ten or so, Smurf King. Maybe they were taken prisoner by the rebels! Or maybe...
Or maybe they've joined their ranks!
Come on! Let's go!
And the small band leaves the Forest in an inglorious retreat.
Ha! Ha! Ha!
Hee! Hee! Hee!
Hey! Here's a gift for you!
Night has fallen. The only bedroom window still lit is that of the Smurf King.
Ten Smurfs missing from formation! And there'll be more...
Unless I smurf the necessary steps.
Heh! Heh! I know what I'm going to do...
S
And the next day.
BLAM
TAGADZAM
BASH
BAMM
Hear ye! To defend the Smurfs against the rebels, the Smurf King has decided to have a protective wall built around the village! All volunteers must smurf to the village square with shovels and pickaxes!
In reward, they will receive another shiny medal!
Pfff!
We've already got one!
Furthermore, all those who don't volunteer will be smurfed into
PRISON!
And speaking of prison...
What are they doing? Just what are they doing?

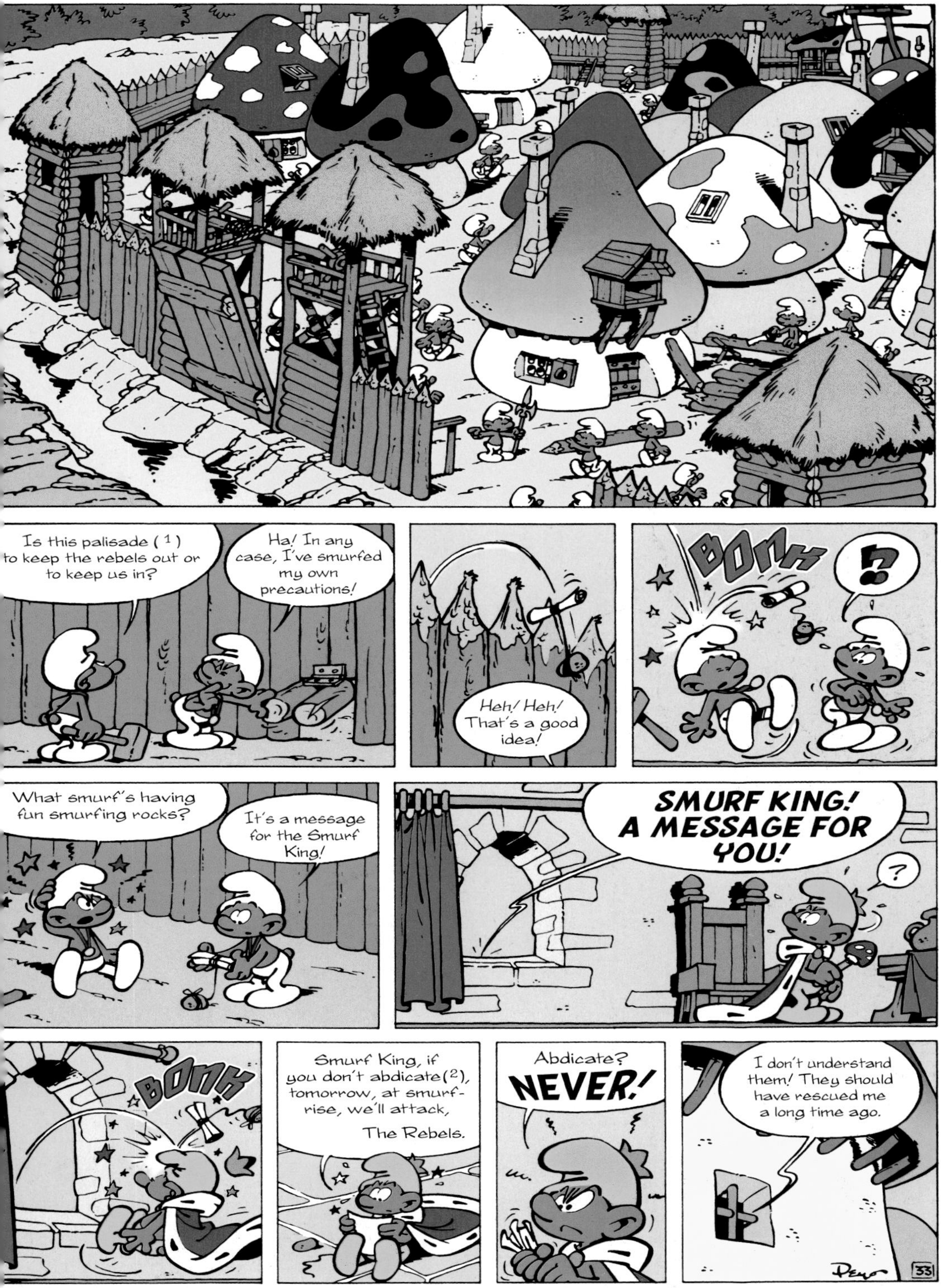

Is this palisade (1) to keep the rebels out or to keep us in?
Ha! In any case, I've smurfed my own precautions!
Heh! Heh! That's a good idea!
BONK
?
What smurf's having fun smurfing rocks?
It's a message for the Smurf King!
SMURF KING! A MESSAGE FOR YOU!
?
BONK
Smurf King, if you don't abdicate(2), tomorrow, at smurf-rise, we'll attack, The Rebels.
Abdicate? NEVER!
I don't understand them! They should have rescued me a long time ago.
33

) Palisade: a fence of pales forming a defense barrier or fortification. (2) Abdicate: to formally give up power. To give up being king, for example.

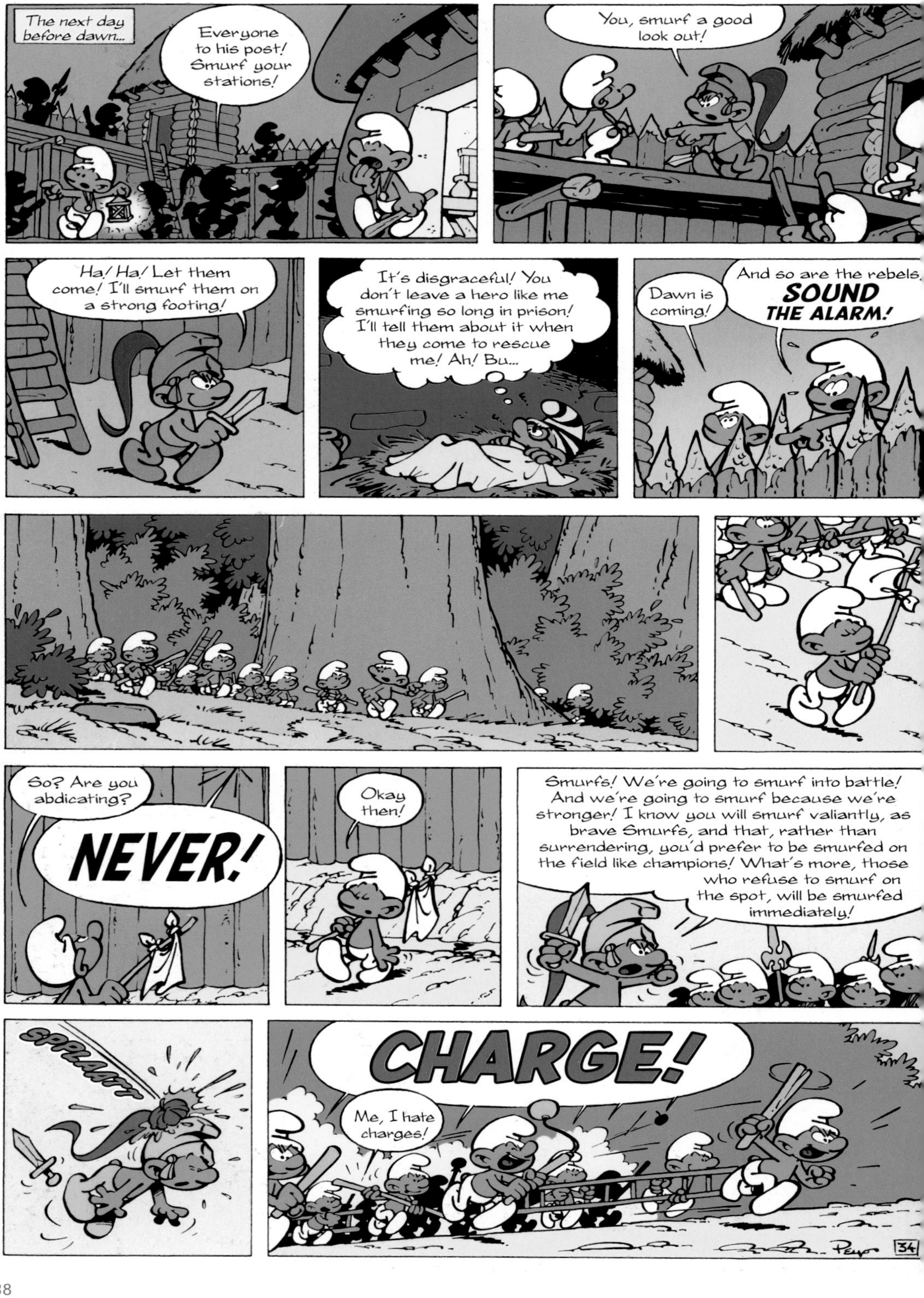
The next day before dawn...
Everyone to his post! Smurf your stations!
You, smurf a good look out!
Ha! Ha! Let them come! I'll smurf them on a strong footing!
It's disgraceful! You don't leave a hero like me smurfing so long in prison! I'll tell them about it when they come to rescue me! Ah! Bu...
Dawn is coming!
And so are the rebels. SOUND THE ALARM!
So? Are you abdicating?
NEVER!
Okay then!
Smurfs! We're going to smurf into battle! And we're going to smurf because we're stronger! I know you will smurf valiantly, as brave Smurfs, and that, rather than surrendering, you'd prefer to be smurfed on the field like champions! What's more, those who refuse to smurf on the spot, will be smurfed immediately!
SPPLAATT
CHARGE!
Me, I hate charges!
Peyo
34

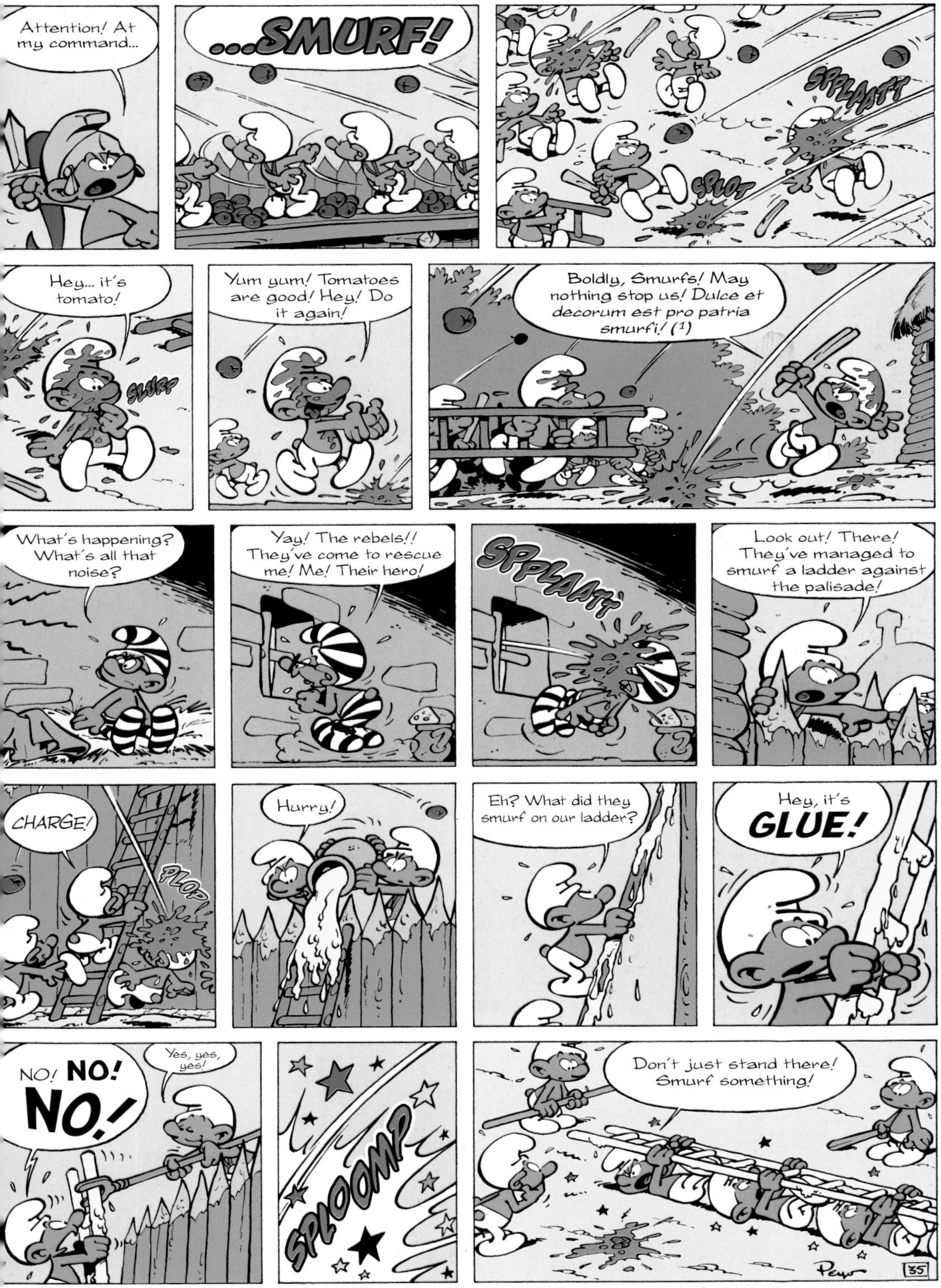
Attention! At my command...
...SMURF!
SPPLAATT
SPLOT
Hey... it's tomato!
SLURP
Yum yum! Tomatoes are good! Hey! Do it again!
Boldly, Smurfs! May nothing stop us! Dulce et decorum est pro patria smurfi! (1)
What's happening? What's all that noise?
Yay! The rebels!! They've come to rescue me! Me! Their hero!
SPPLAATT
Look out! There! They've managed to smurf a ladder against the palisade!
CHARGE!
PLOP
Hurry!
Eh? What did they smurf on our ladder?
Hey, it's GLUE!
NO! NO! NO!
Yes, yes, yes!
SPLOOMP
Don't just stand there! Smurf something!
Peyo
35

(1) A famous line by Roman poet Horace, in Latin (and Smurf) for: "It is sweet and right to die for your country."

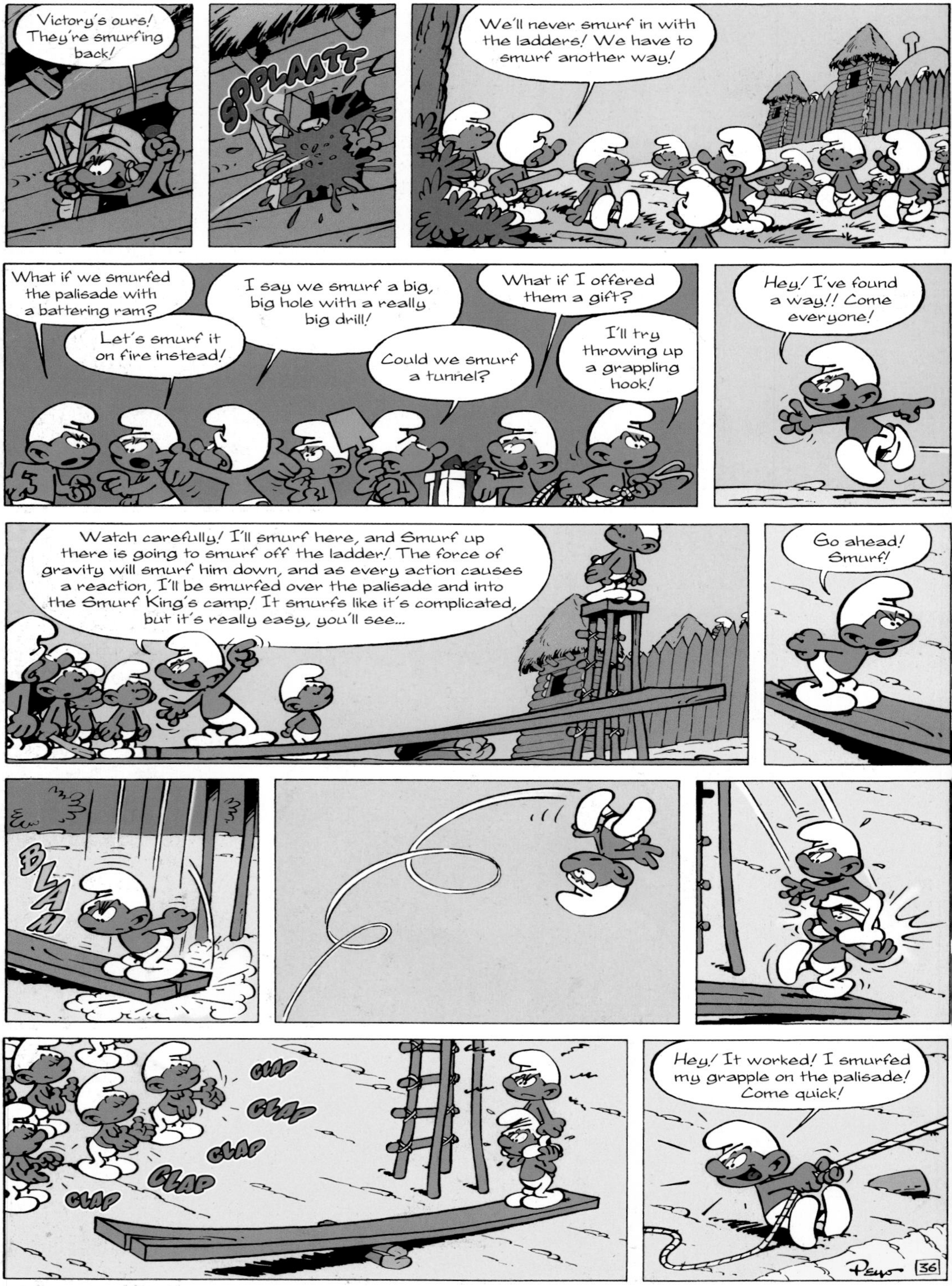

Victory's ours! They're smurfing back!
SPPLAATT
We'll never smurf in with the ladders! We have to smurf another way!
What if we smurfed the palisade with a battering ram?
Let's smurf it on fire instead!
I say we smurf a big, big hole with a really big drill!
Could we smurf a tunnel?
What if I offered them a gift?
I'll try throwing up a grappling hook!
Hey! I've found a way!! Come everyone!
Watch carefully! I'll smurf here, and Smurf up there is going to smurf off the ladder! The force of gravity will smurf him down, and as every action causes a reaction, I'll be smurfed over the palisade and into the Smurf King's camp! It smurfs like it's complicated, but it's really easy, you'll see...
Go ahead! Smurf!
BLAM
CLAP
CLAP
CLAP
CLAP
CLAP
Hey! It worked! I smurfed my grapple on the palisade! Come quick!
36

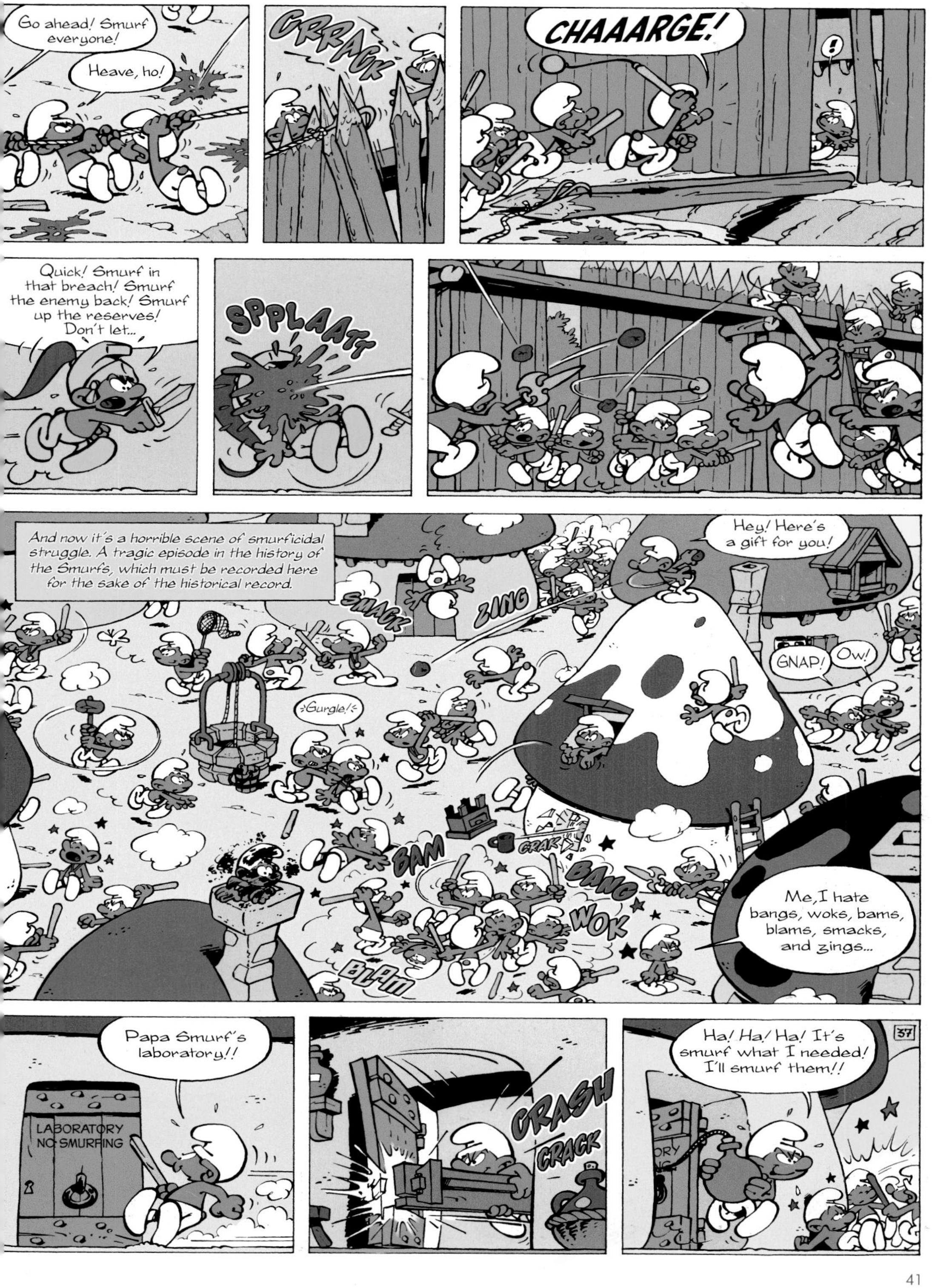

Go ahead! Smurf everyone!
Heave, ho!
CRRACK
CHAAARGE!
!
Quick! Smurf in that breach! Smurf the enemy back! Smurf up the reserves! Don't let...
SPPLAATT
And now it's a horrible scene of smurficidal struggle. A tragic episode in the history of the Smurfs, which must be recorded here for the sake of the historical record.
Hey! Here's a gift for you!
SMACK
ZING
GNAP!
Ow!
Gurgle!
BAM
CRAK
BANG
WOK
BLAM
Me, I hate bangs, woks, bams, blams, smacks, and zings...
Papa Smurf's laboratory!!
LABORATORY NO SMURFING
CRASH
CRACK
Ha! Ha! Ha! It's smurf what I needed! I'll smurf them!!
37

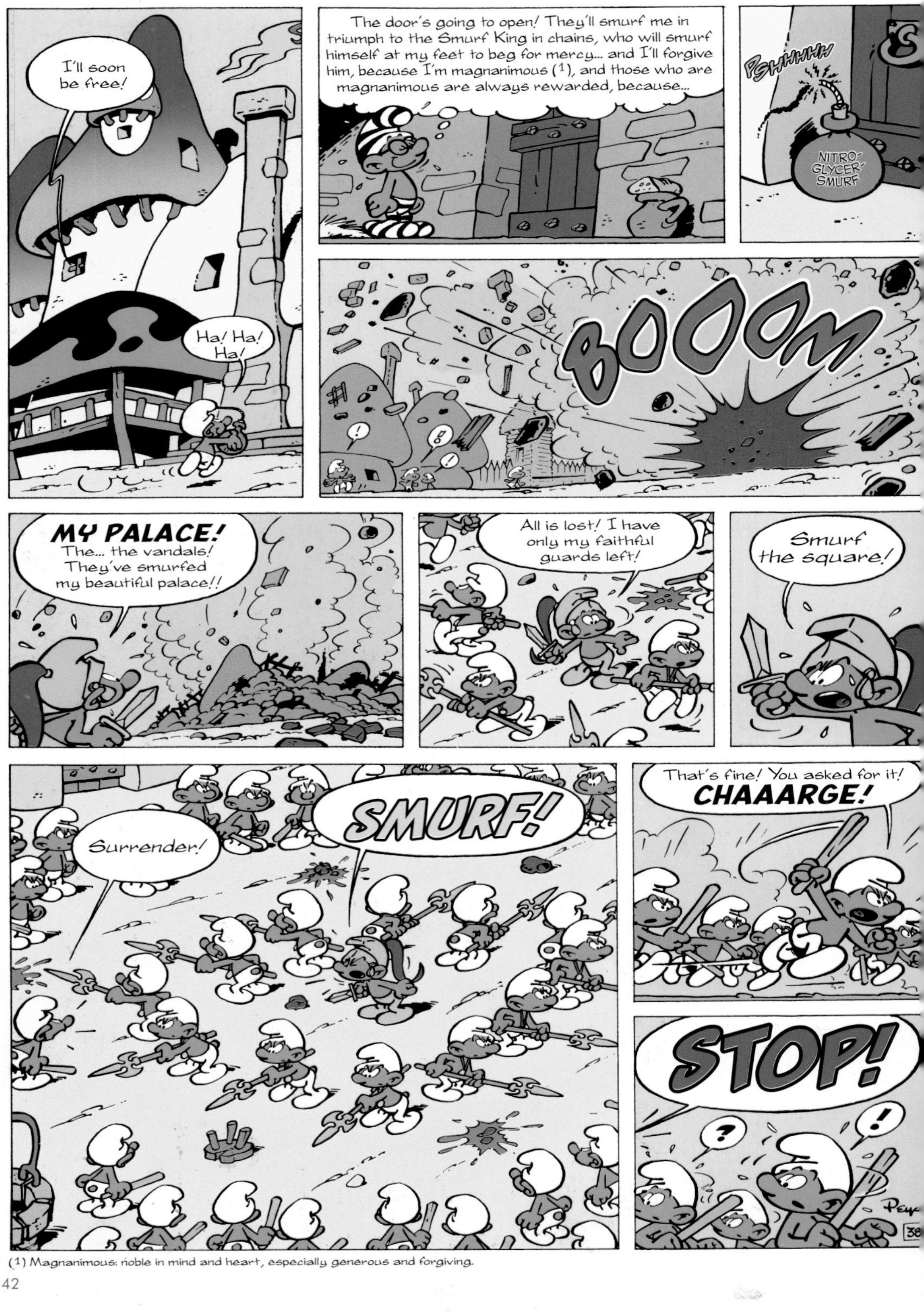

I'll soon be free!
Ha! Ha! Ha!
The door's going to open! They'll smurf me in triumph to the Smurf King in chains, who will smurf himself at my feet to beg for mercy... and I'll forgive him, because I'm magnanimous (1), and those who are magnanimous are always rewarded, because...
PSHHHHH
NITRO-GLYCER-SMURF
BOOOM
MY PALACE! The... the vandals! They've smurfed my beautiful palace!!
All is lost! I have only my faithful guards left!
Smurf the square!
Surrender!
SMURF!
That's fine! You asked for it! CHAAARGE!
STOP!
?
!

(1) Magnanimous: noble in mind and heart, especially generous and forgiving.

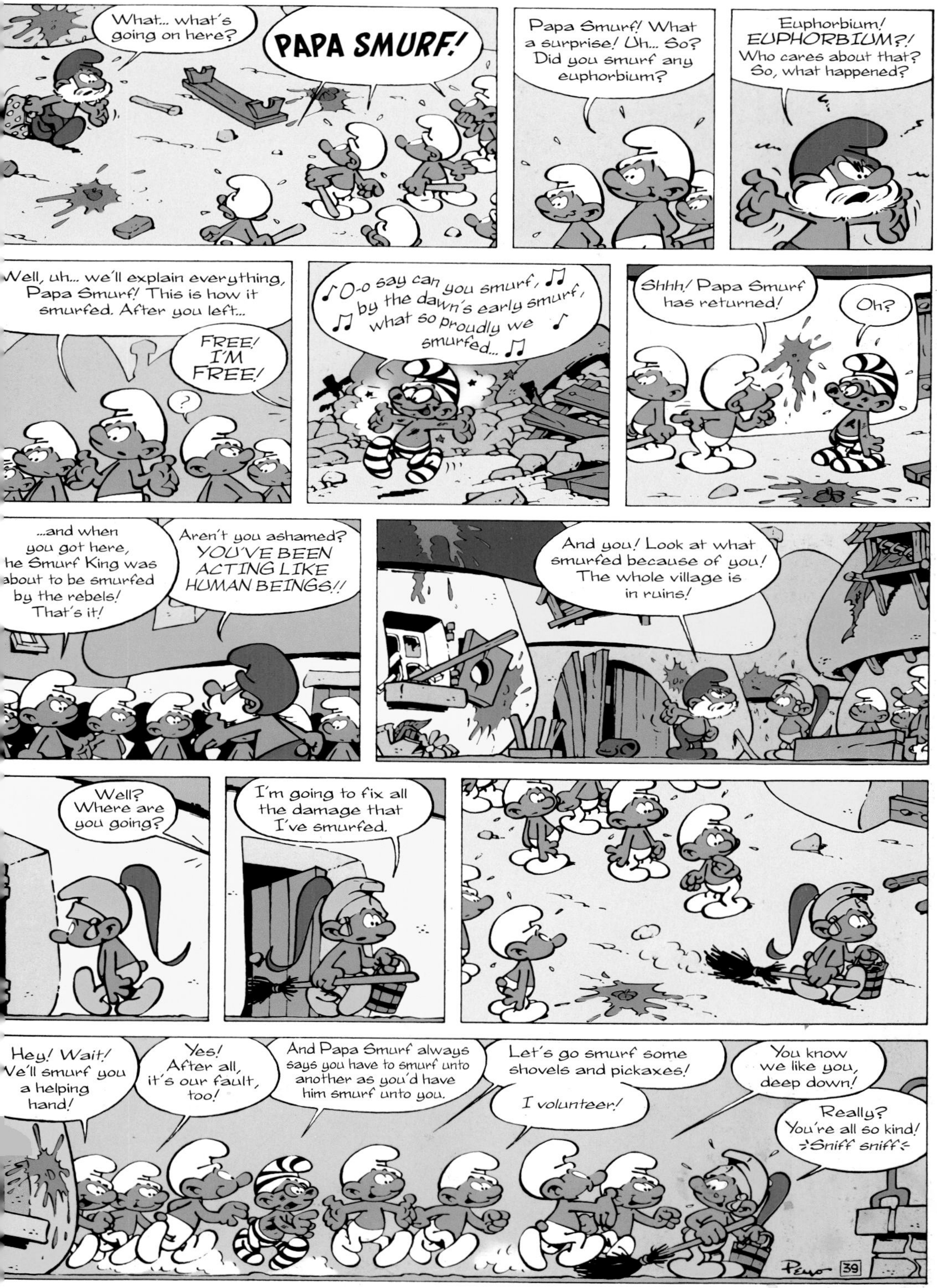
What... what's going on here?
PAPA SMURF!
Papa Smurf! What a surprise! Uh... So? Did you smurf any euphorbium?
Euphorbium! EUPHORBIUM?! Who cares about that? So, what happened?
Well, uh... we'll explain everything, Papa Smurf! This is how it smurfed. After you left...
FREE! I'M FREE!
?
O-o say can you smurf, by the dawn's early smurf, what so proudly we smurfed...
Shhh! Papa Smurf has returned!
Oh?
...and when you got here, he Smurf King was about to be smurfed by the rebels! That's it!
Aren't you ashamed? YOU'VE BEEN ACTING LIKE HUMAN BEINGS!!
And you! Look at what smurfed because of you! The whole village is in ruins!
Well? Where are you going?
I'm going to fix all the damage that I've smurfed.
Hey! Wait! Ve'll smurf you a helping hand!
Yes! After all, it's our fault, too!
And Papa Smurf always says you have to smurf unto another as you'd have him smurf unto you.
Let's go smurf some shovels and pickaxes!
I volunteer!
You know we like you, deep down!
Really? You're all so kind! Sniff sniff
Peyo
39

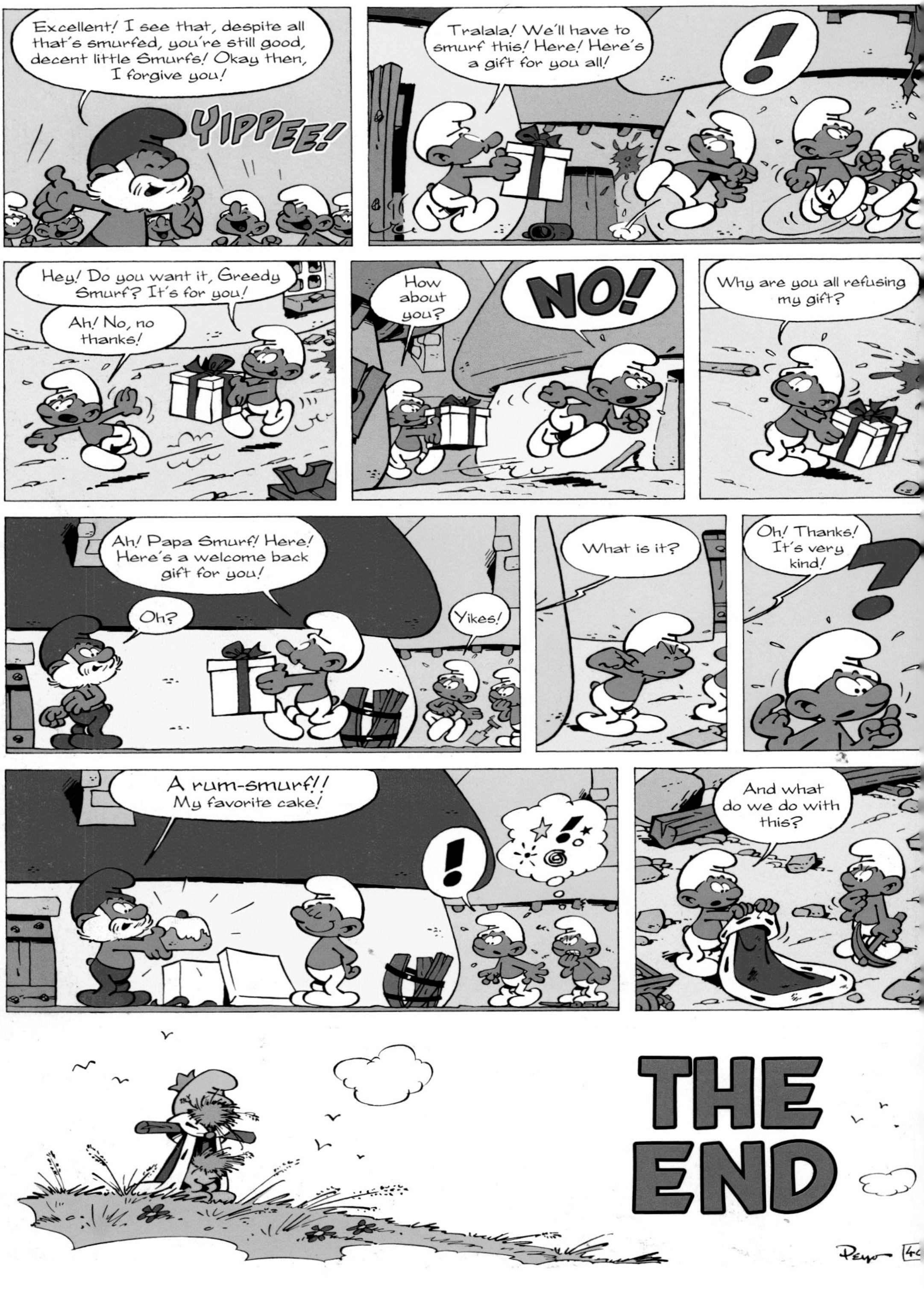
Excellent! I see that, despite all that's smurfed, you're still good, decent little Smurfs! Okay then, I forgive you!
YIPPEE!
Tralala! We'll have to smurf this! Here! Here's a gift for you all!
!
Hey! Do you want it, Greedy Smurf? It's for you!
Ah! No, no thanks!
How about you?
NO!
Why are you all refusing my gift?
Ah! Papa Smurf! Here! Here's a welcome back gift for you!
Oh?
Yikes!
What is it?
Oh! Thanks! It's very kind!
?
A rum-smurf!! My favorite cake!
!
And what do we do with this?
THE END
Peyo

THE SMURFONY

By Peyo and YVAN DELPORTE

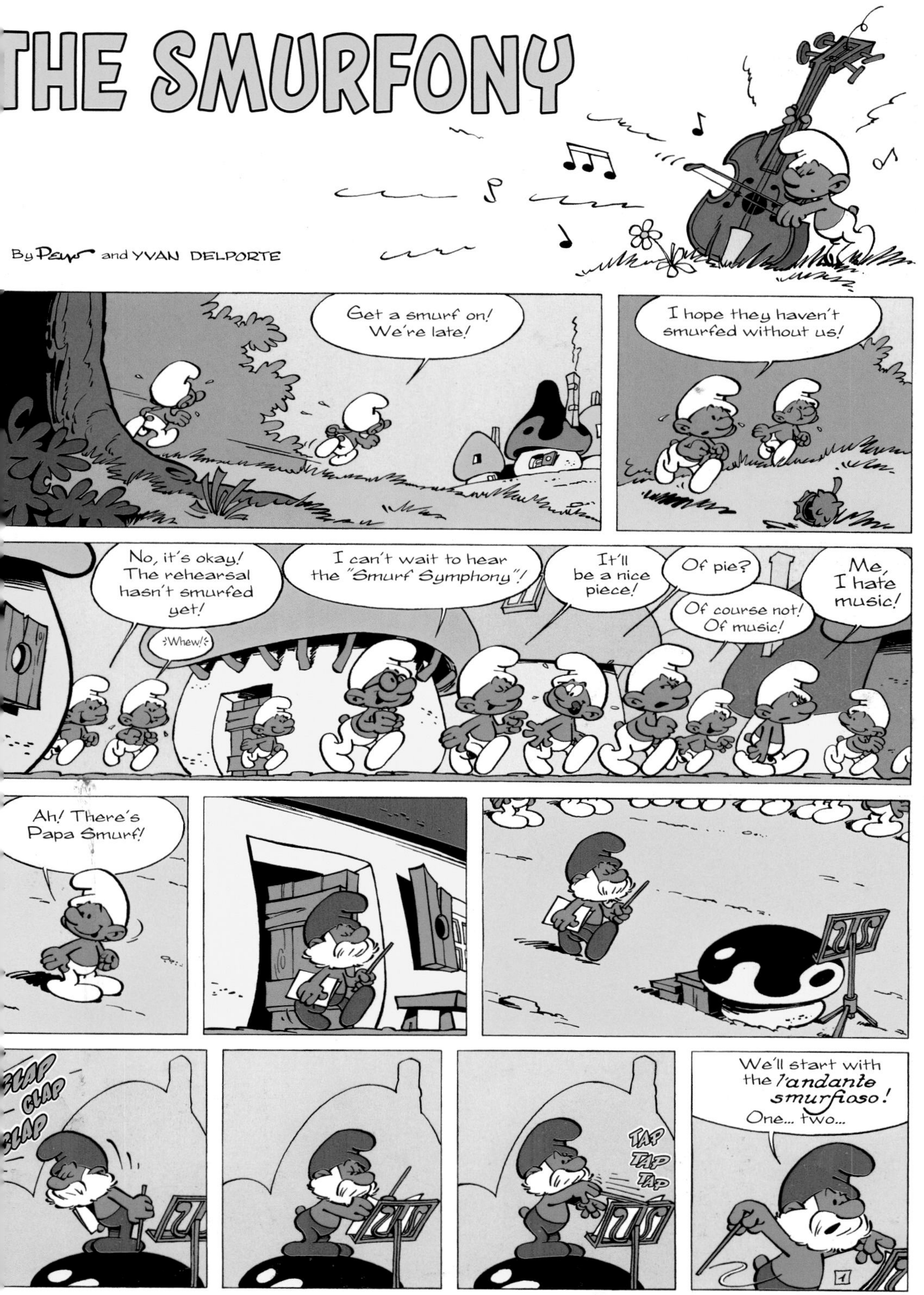

Get a smurf on! We're late!
I hope they haven't smurfed without us!
No, it's okay! The rehearsal hasn't smurfed yet!
Whew!
I can't wait to hear the "Smurf Symphony"!
It'll be a nice piece!
Of pie?
Of course not! Of music!
Me, I hate music!
Ah! There's Papa Smurf!
CLAP CLAP CLAP
TAP TAP TAP
We'll start with the l'andante smurfioso! One... two...
1

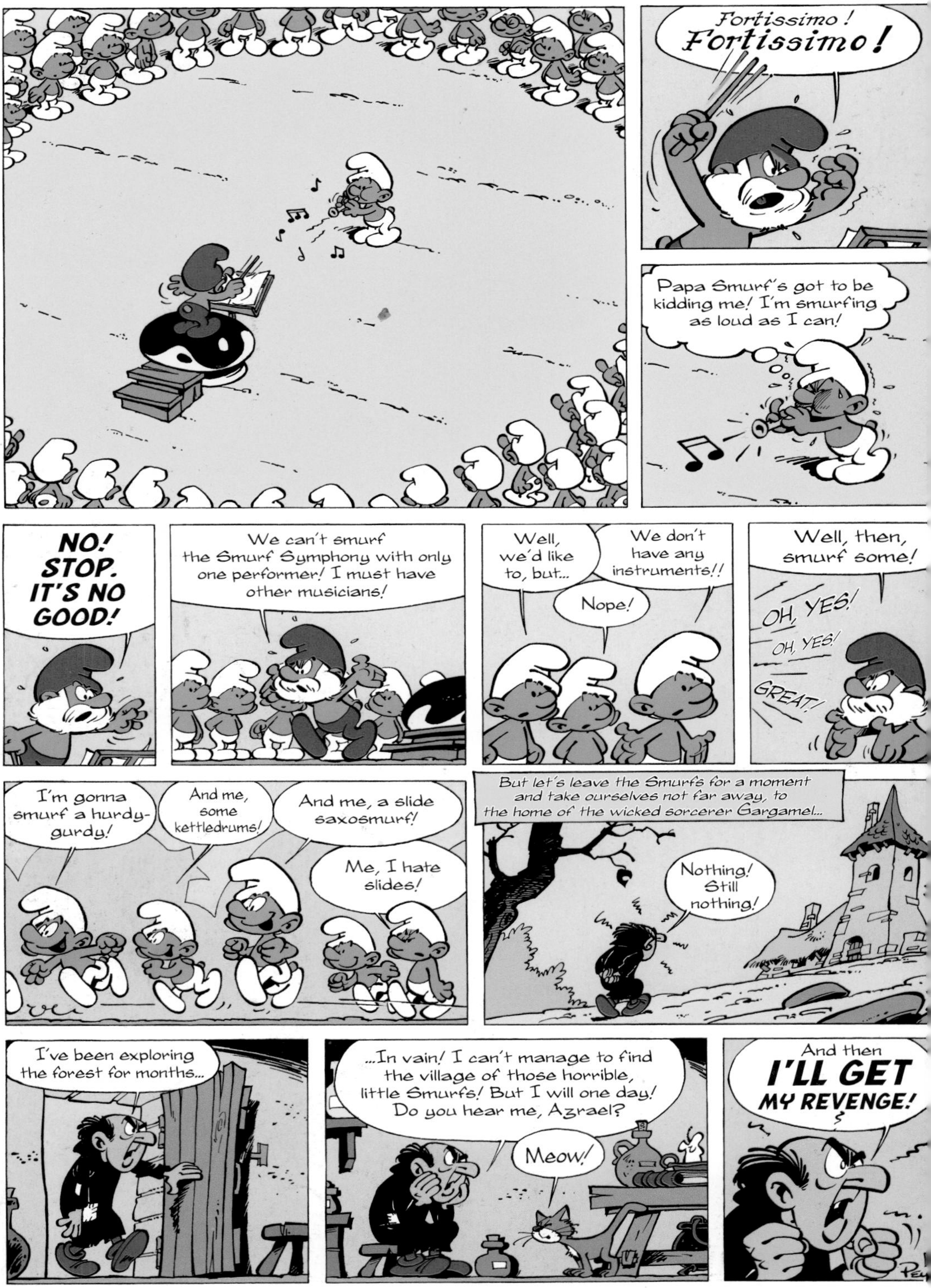
Fortissimo!
Fortissimo!
Papa Smurf's got to be kidding me! I'm smurfing as loud as I can!
NO! STOP. IT'S NO GOOD!
We can't smurf the Smurf Symphony with only one performer! I must have other musicians!
Well, we'd like to, but...
We don't have any instruments!!
Nope!
Well, then, smurf some!
OH, YES!
OH, YES!
GREAT!
I'm gonna smurf a hurdy-gurdy!
And me, some kettledrums!
And me, a slide saxosmurf!
Me, I hate slides!
But let's leave the Smurfs for a moment and take ourselves not far away, to the home of the wicked sorcerer Gargamel...
Nothing! Still nothing!
I've been exploring the forest for months...
...In vain! I can't manage to find the village of those horrible, little Smurfs! But I will one day! Do you hear me, Azrael?
Meow!
And then I'LL GET MY REVENGE!

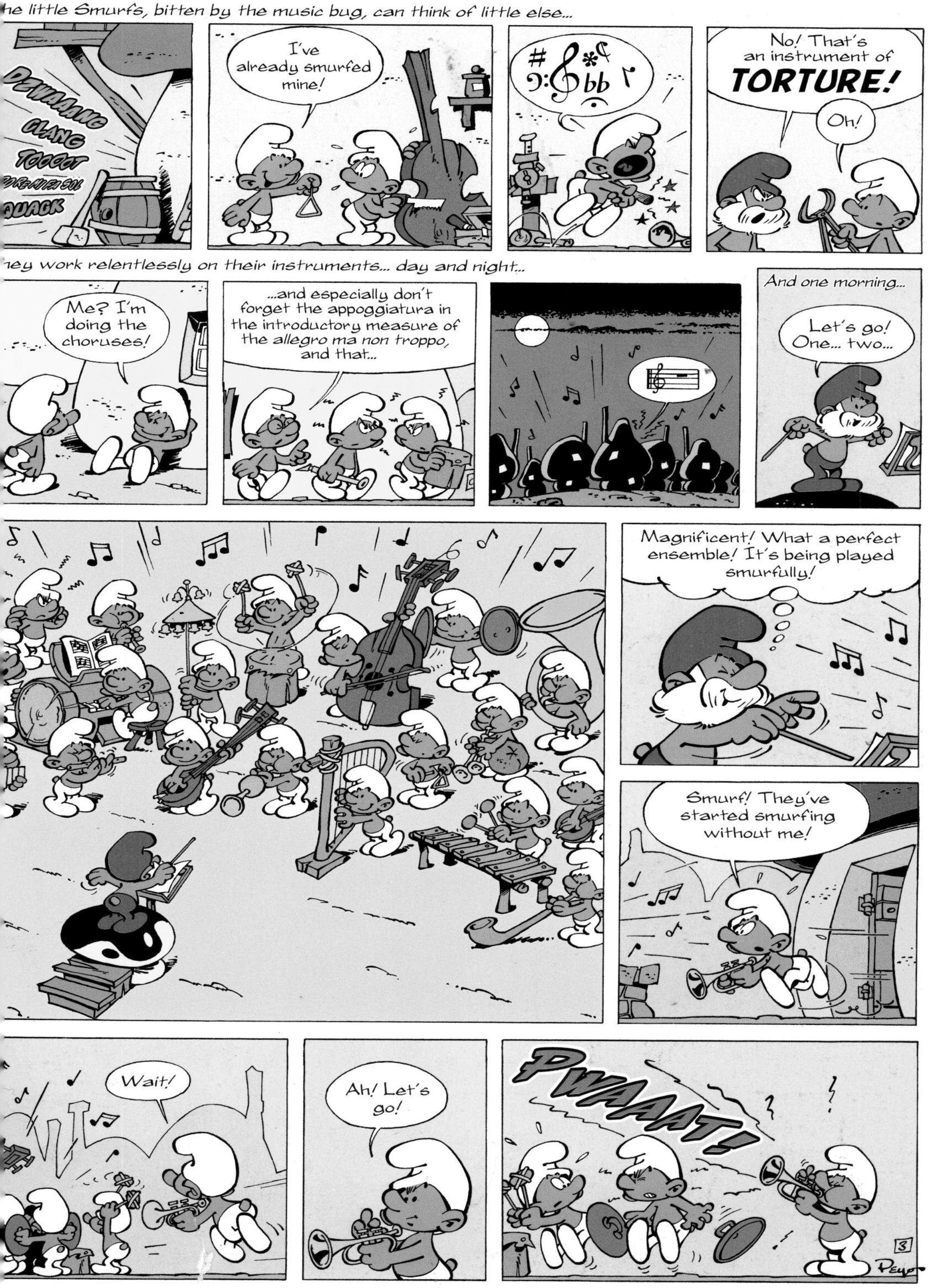
he little Smurfs, bitten by the music bug, can think of little else...
DZWAAANG
CLANG
TOOOOT
RE-MI-FA SOL
UACK
I've already smurfed mine!
No! That's an instrument of TORTURE!
Oh!
hey work relentlessly on their instruments... day and night...
Me? I'm doing the choruses!
...and especially don't forget the appoggiatura in the introductory measure of the allegro ma non troppo, and that...
And one morning...
Let's go! One... two...
Magnificent! What a perfect ensemble! It's being played smurfully!
Smurf! They've started smurfing without me!
Wait!
Ah! Let's go!
PWAAAT!
3
Peyo

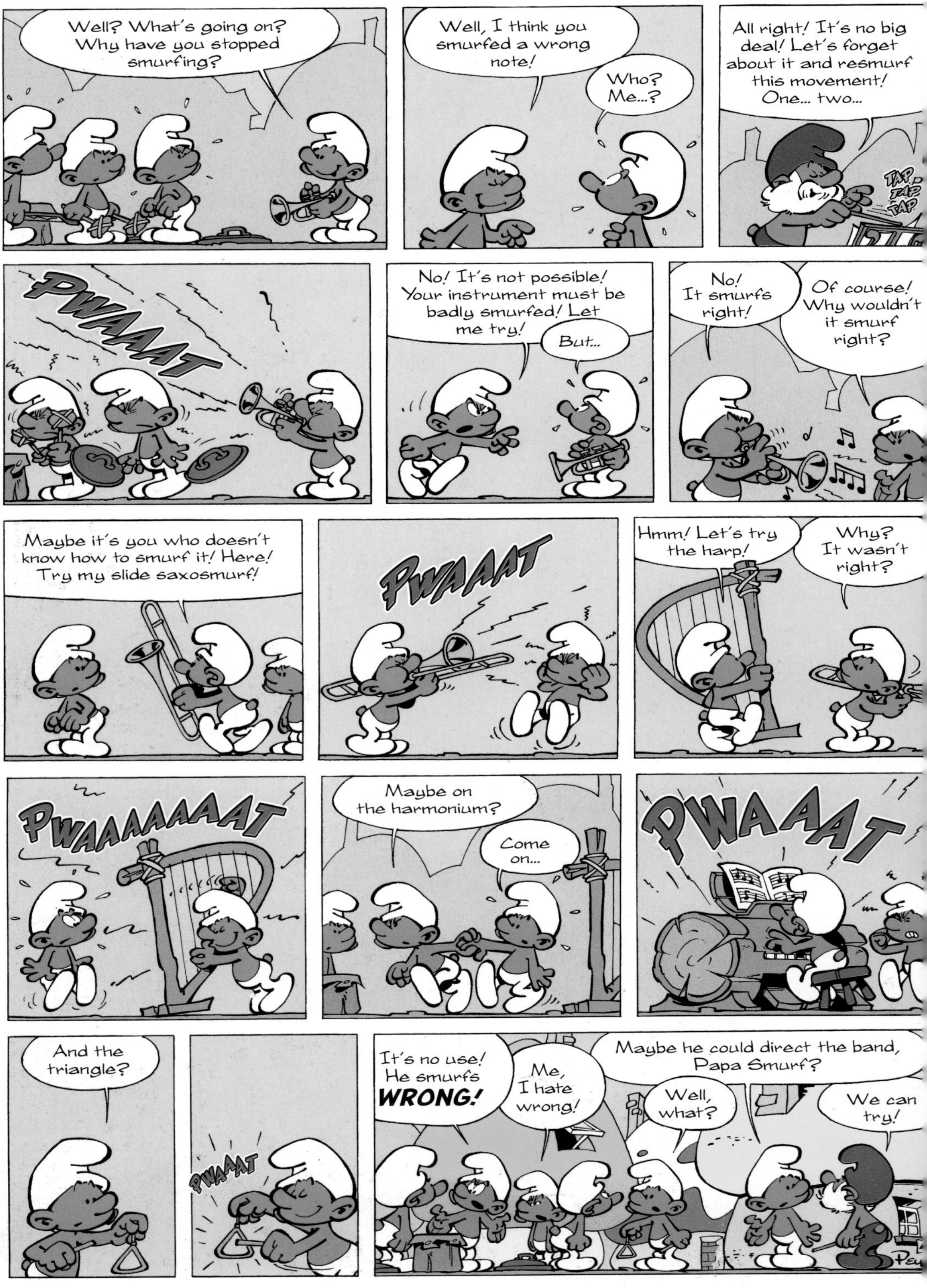

Well? What's going on? Why have you stopped smurfing?
Well, I think you smurfed a wrong note!
Who? Me...?
All right! It's no big deal! Let's forget about it and resmurf this movement! One... two...
TAP TAP TAP
PWAAAT
No! It's not possible! Your instrument must be badly smurfed! Let me try!
But...
No! It smurfs right!
Of course! Why wouldn't it smurf right?
Maybe it's you who doesn't know how to smurf it! Here! Try my slide saxosmurf!
PWAAAT
Hmm! Let's try the harp!
Why? It wasn't right?
PWAAAAAAAT
Maybe on the harmonium?
Come on...
PWAAAT
And the triangle?
PWAAAT
It's no use! He smurfs WRONG!
Me, I hate wrong!
Maybe he could direct the band, Papa Smurf?
Well, what?
We can try!

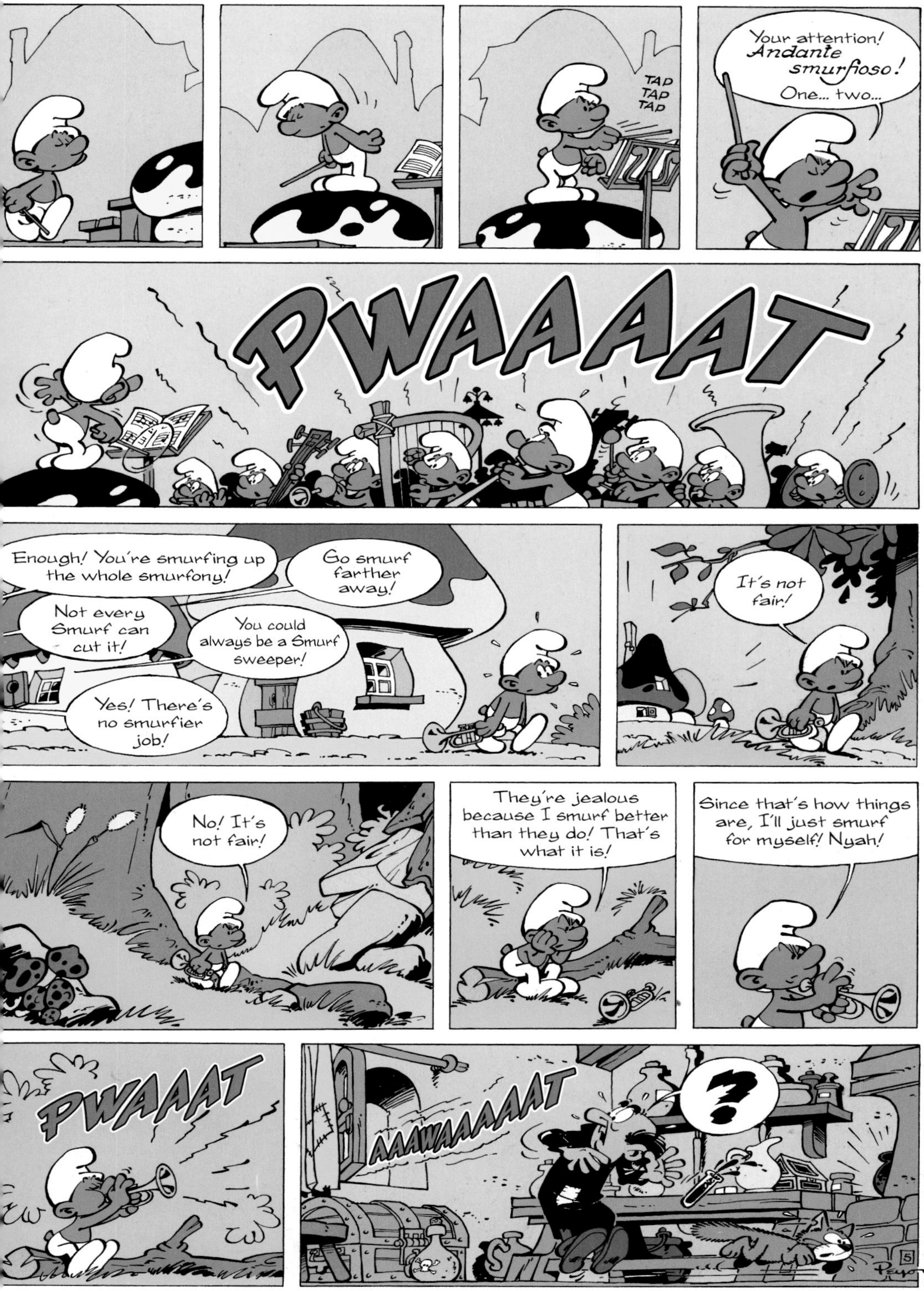
TAP
TAP
TAP
Your attention! Andante smurfioso! One... two...
PWAAAAT
Enough! You're smurfing up the whole smurfony!
Go smurf farther away!
Not every Smurf can cut it!
You could always be a Smurf sweeper!
Yes! There's no smurfier job!
It's not fair!
No! It's not fair!
They're jealous because I smurf better than they do! That's what it is!
Since that's how things are, I'll just smurf for myself! Nyah!
PWAAAT
AAAWAAAAAAT
?
5
Peyo

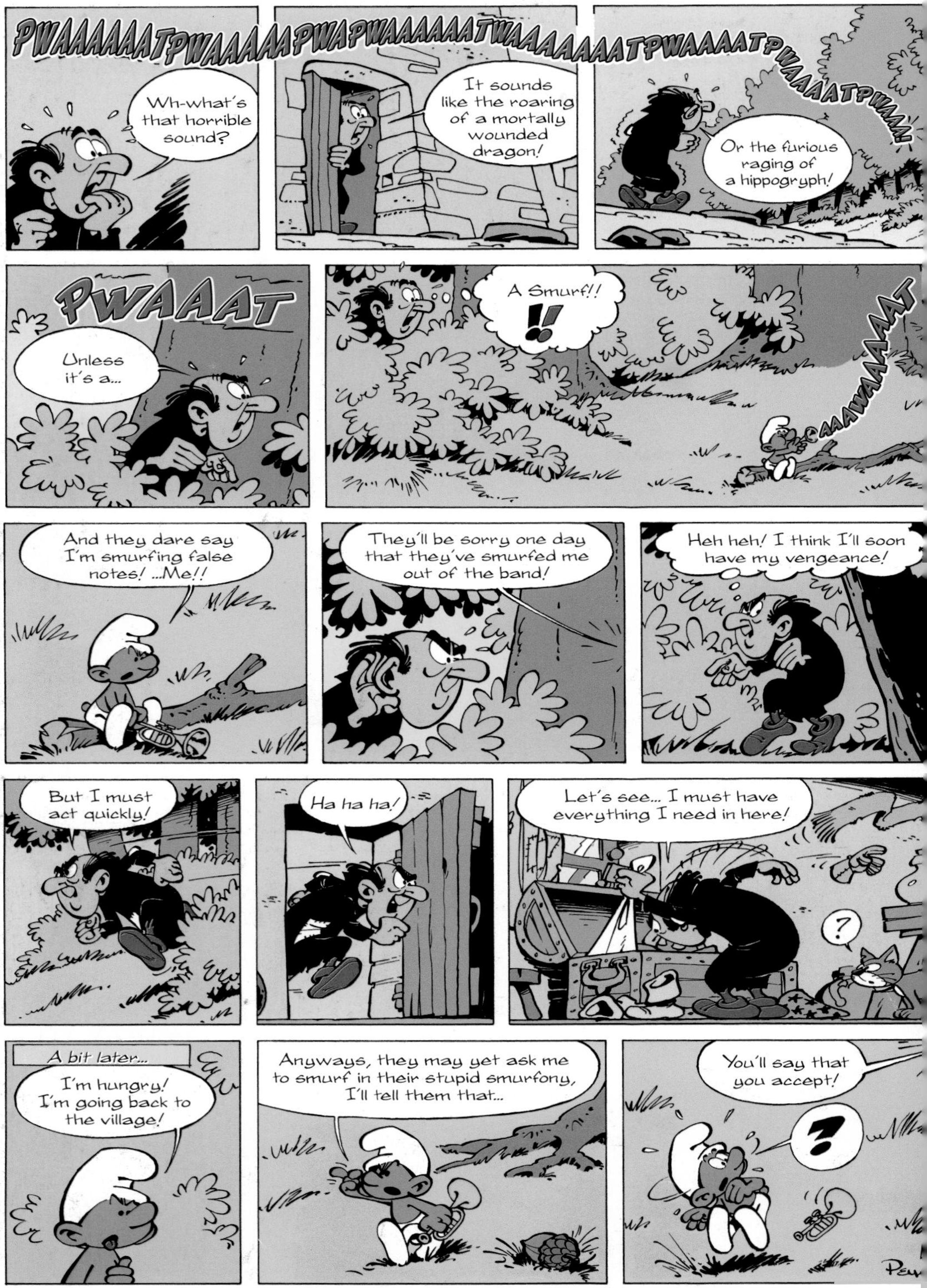
PWAAAAAATPWAAAAAPWAPWAAAAAAATWAAAAAAAATPWAAAATPWAAAAATPWAAA!
Wh-what's that horrible sound?
It sounds like the roaring of a mortally wounded dragon!
Or the furious raging of a hippogryph!
PWAAAT
Unless it's a...
A Smurf!!
!!
And they dare say I'm smurfing false notes! ...Me!!
They'll be sorry one day that they've smurfed me out of the band!
Heh heh! I think I'll soon have my vengeance!
But I must act quickly!
Ha ha ha!
Let's see... I must have everything I need in here!
?
A bit later...
I'm hungry! I'm going back to the village!
Anyways, they may yet ask me to smurf in their stupid smurfony, I'll tell them that...
You'll say that you accept!
?

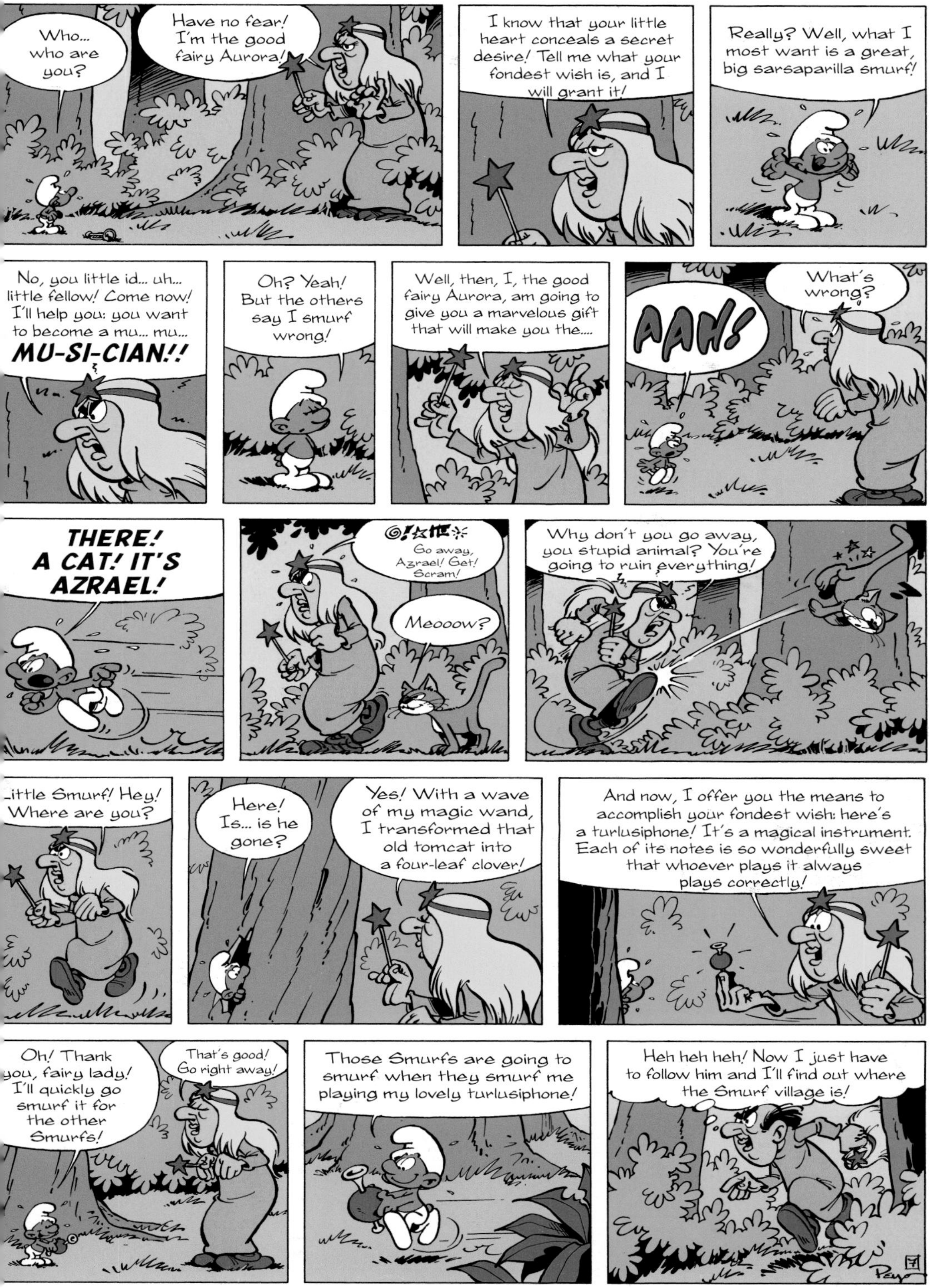

Who... who are you?
Have no fear! I'm the good fairy Aurora!
I know that your little heart conceals a secret desire! Tell me what your fondest wish is, and I will grant it!
Really? Well, what I most want is a great, big sarsaparilla smurf!
No, you little id... uh... little fellow! Come now! I'll help you: you want to become a mu... mu... MU-SI-CIAN!!
Oh? Yeah! But the others say I smurf wrong!
Well, then, I, the good fairy Aurora, am going to give you a marvelous gift that will make you the....
AAH!
What's wrong?
THERE! A CAT! IT'S AZRAEL!
Go away, Azrael! Get! Scram!
Meooow?
Why don't you go away, you stupid animal? You're going to ruin everything!
Little Smurf! Hey! Where are you?
Here! Is... is he gone?
Yes! With a wave of my magic wand, I transformed that old tomcat into a four-leaf clover!
And now, I offer you the means to accomplish your fondest wish: here's a turlusiphone! It's a magical instrument. Each of its notes is so wonderfully sweet that whoever plays it always plays correctly!
Oh! Thank you, fairy lady! I'll quickly go smurf it for the other Smurfs!
That's good! Go right away!
Those Smurfs are going to smurf when they smurf me playing my lovely turlusiphone!
Heh heh heh! Now I just have to follow him and I'll find out where the Smurf village is!

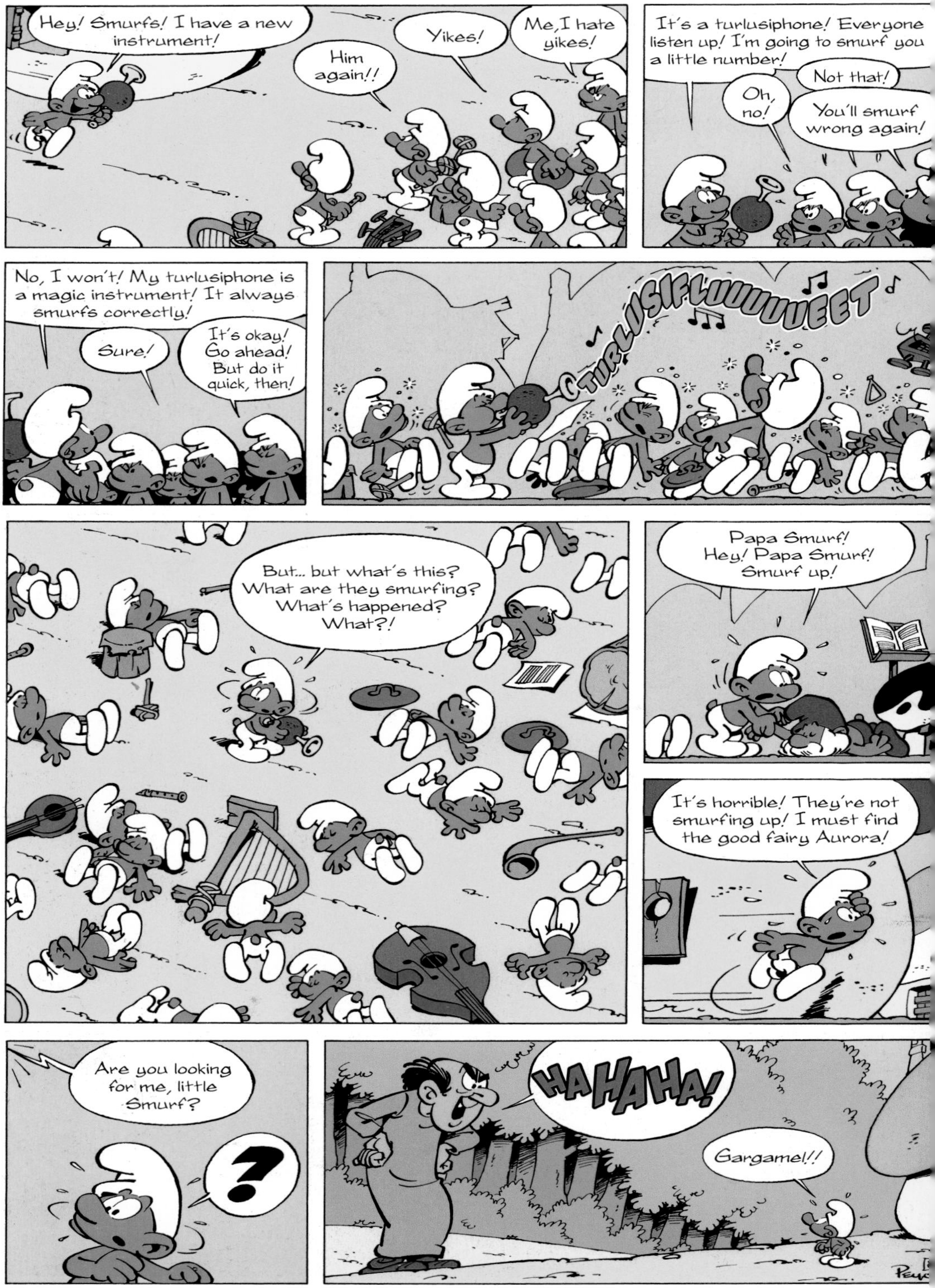

Hey! Smurfs! I have a new instrument!
Him again!!
Yikes!
Me, I hate yikes!
It's a turlusiphone! Everyone listen up! I'm going to smurf you a little number!
Oh, no!
Not that!
You'll smurf wrong again!
No, I won't! My turlusiphone is a magic instrument! It always smurfs correctly!
Sure!
It's okay! Go ahead! But do it quick, then!
TURLUSIFLUUUUUVEET
But... but what's this? What are they smurfing? What's happened? What?!
Papa Smurf! Hey! Papa Smurf! Smurf up!
It's horrible! They're not smurfing up! I must find the good fairy Aurora!
Are you looking for me, little Smurf?
?
HAHAHAHA!
Gargamel!!

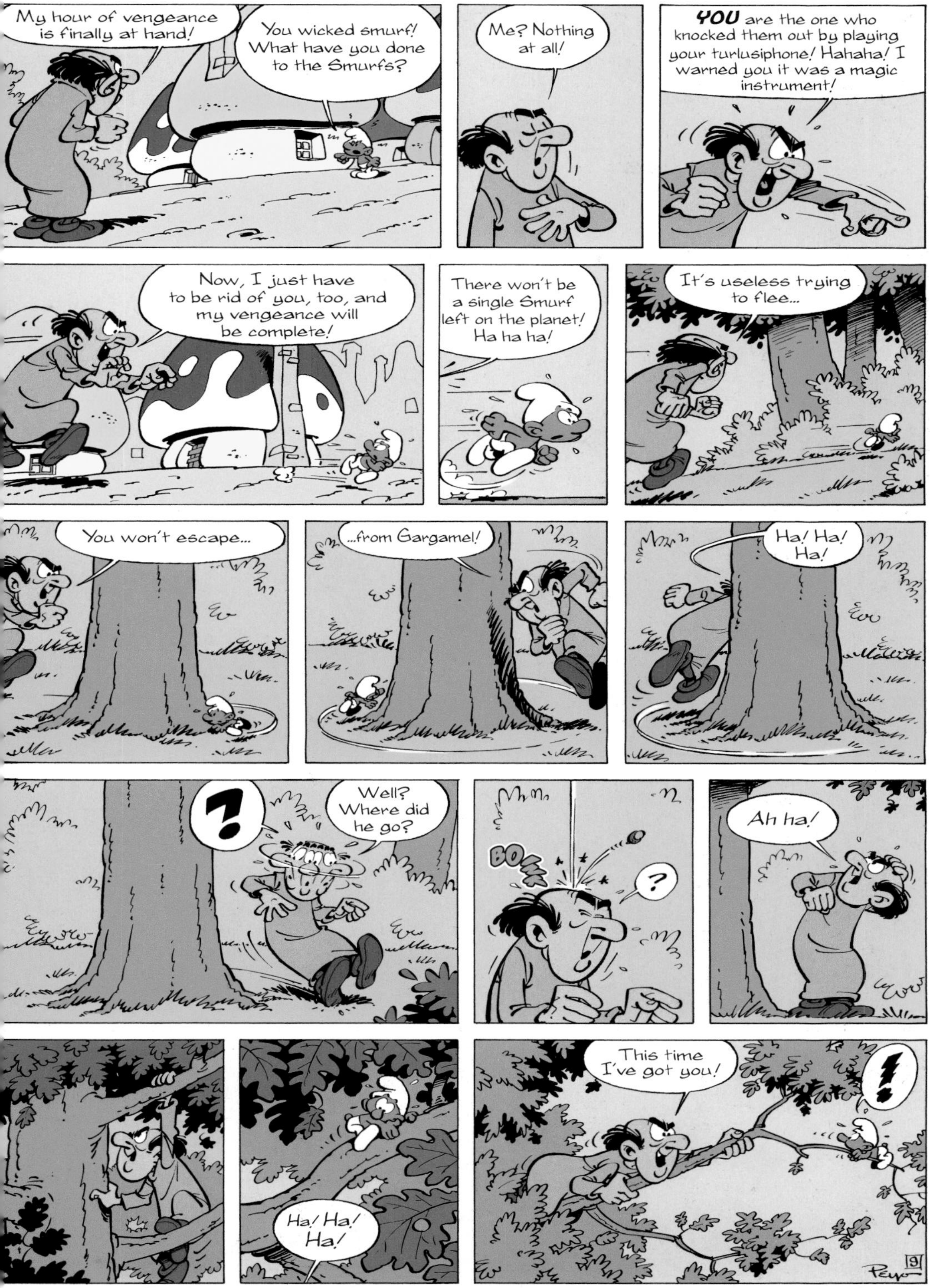
My hour of vengeance is finally at hand!
You wicked smurf! What have you done to the Smurfs?
Me? Nothing at all!
YOU are the one who knocked them out by playing your turlusiphone! Hahaha! I warned you it was a magic instrument!
Now, I just have to be rid of you, too, and my vengeance will be complete!
There won't be a single Smurf left on the planet! Ha ha ha!
It's useless trying to flee...
You won't escape...
...from Gargamel!
Ha! Ha! Ha!
Well? Where did he go?
BOK
?
Ah ha!
Ha! Ha! Ha!
This time I've got you!
9

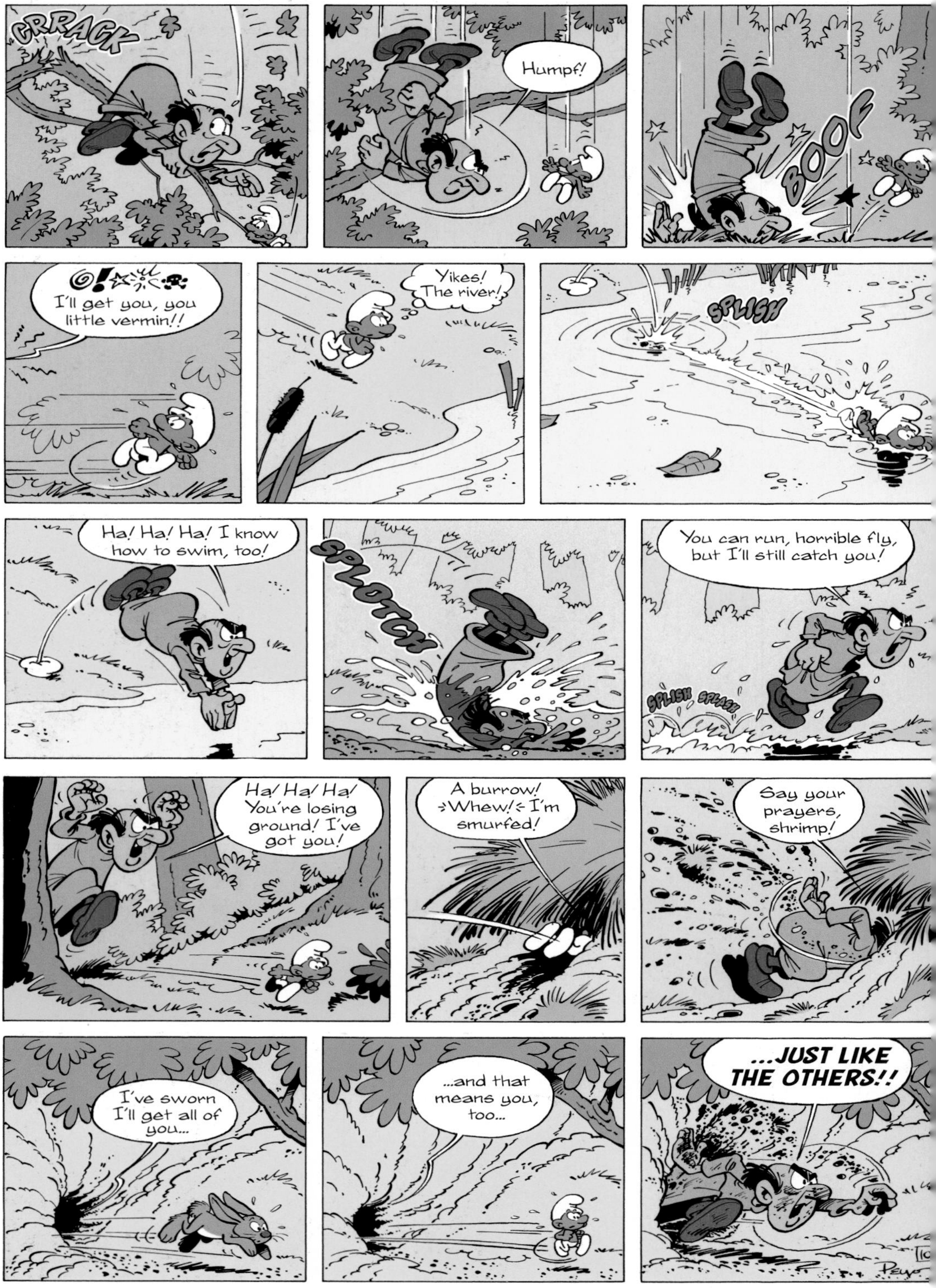
CRRACK
Humpf!
BOOF
I'll get you, you little vermin!!
Yikes! The river!
SPLISH
Ha! Ha! Ha! I know how to swim, too!
SPLOTCH
You can run, horrible fly, but I'll still catch you!
SPLISH SPLASH
Ha! Ha! Ha! You're losing ground! I've got you!
A burrow! Whew! I'm smurfed!
Say your prayers, shrimp!
I've sworn I'll get all of you...
...and that means you, too...
...JUST LIKE THE OTHERS!!
Peyo

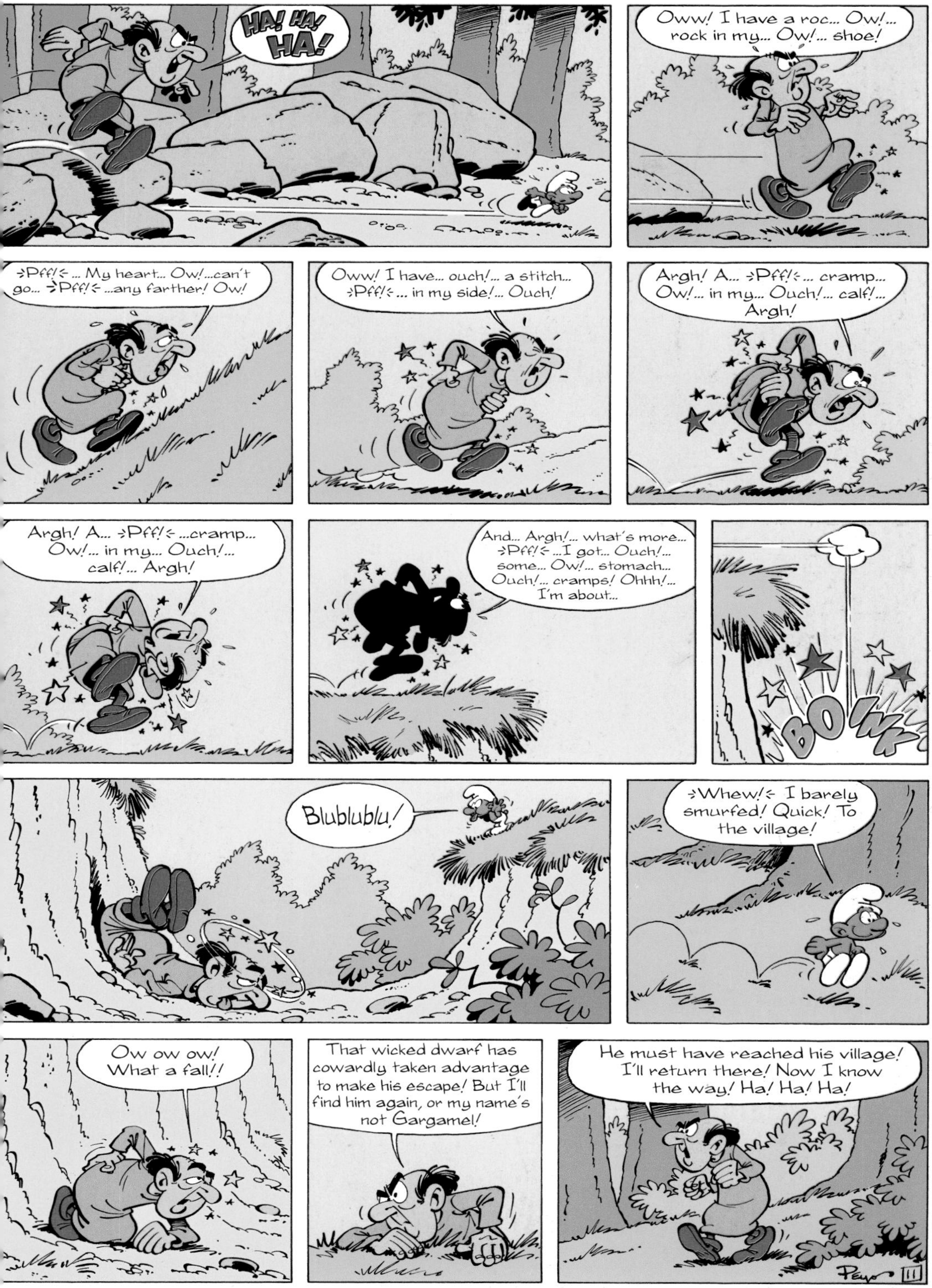
HA! HA! HA!
Oww! I have a roc... Ow!... rock in my... Ow!... shoe!
→Pff!← ... My heart... Ow!...can't go... →Pff!← ...any farther! Ow!
Oww! I have... ouch!... a stitch... →Pff!← ... in my side!... Ouch!
Argh! A... →Pff!← ... cramp... Ow!... in my... Ouch!... calf!... Argh!
Argh! A... →Pff!← ...cramp... Ow!... in my... Ouch!... calf!... Argh!
And... Argh!... what's more... →Pff!← ...I got... Ouch!... some... Ow!... stomach... Ouch!... cramps! Ohhh!... I'm about...
BOINK
Blublublu!
→Whew!← I barely smurfed! Quick! To the village!
Ow ow ow! What a fall!!
That wicked dwarf has cowardly taken advantage to make his escape! But I'll find him again, or my name's not Gargamel!
He must have reached his village! I'll return there! Now I know the way! Ha! Ha! Ha!
Peyo III

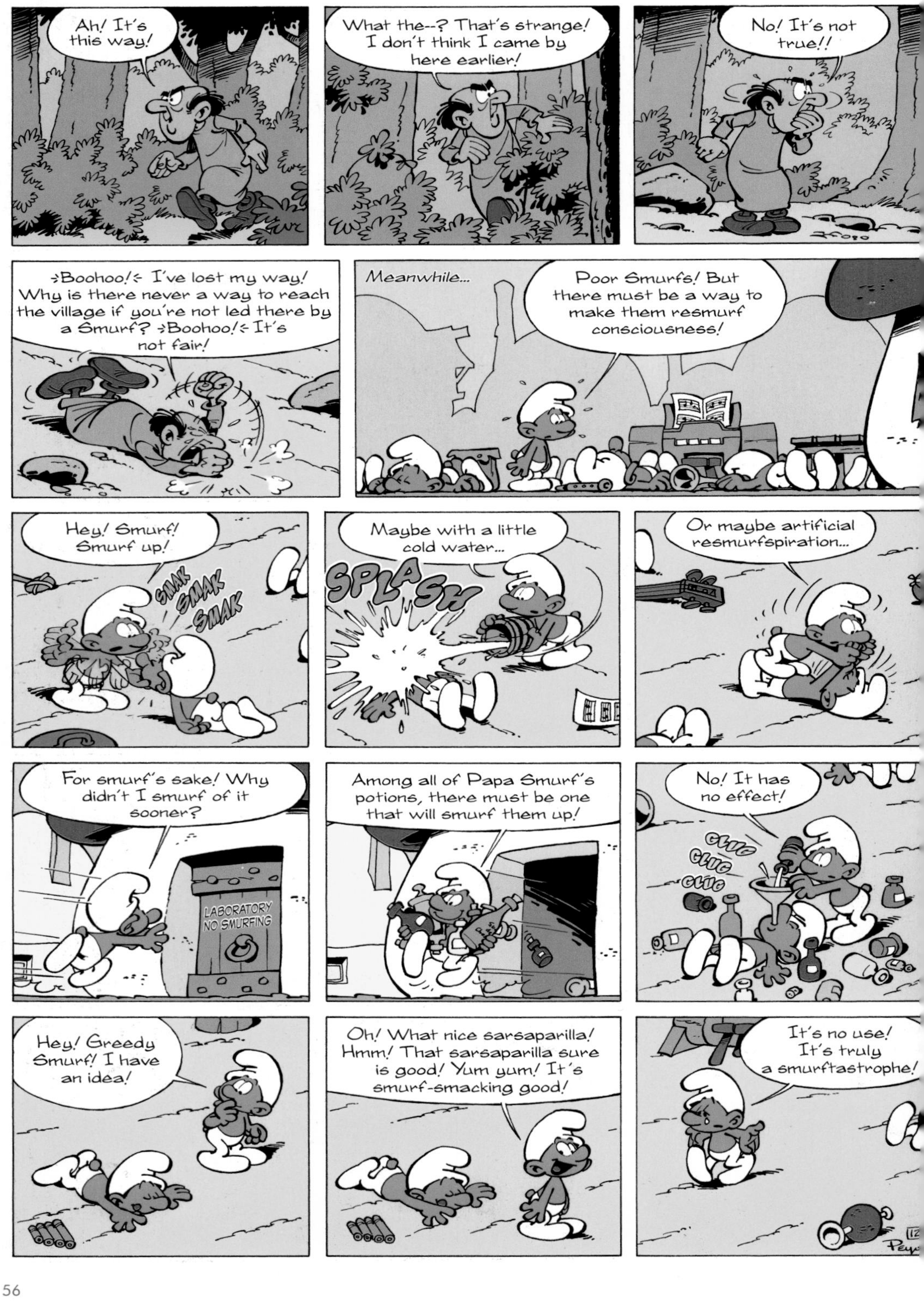
Ah! It's this way!
What the--? That's strange! I don't think I came by here earlier!
No! It's not true!!
>Boohoo!< I've lost my way! Why is there never a way to reach the village if you're not led there by a Smurf? >Boohoo!< It's not fair!
Meanwhile...
Poor Smurfs! But there must be a way to make them resmurf consciousness!
Hey! Smurf! Smurf up!
SMAK SMAK SMAK
Maybe with a little cold water...
SPLASH
Or maybe artificial resmurfspiration...
For smurf's sake! Why didn't I smurf of it sooner?
LABORATORY NO SMURFING
Among all of Papa Smurf's potions, there must be one that will smurf them up!
No! It has no effect!
GLUG GLUG GLUG
Hey! Greedy Smurf! I have an idea!
Oh! What nice sarsaparilla! Hmm! That sarsaparilla sure is good! Yum yum! It's smurf-smacking good!
It's no use! It's truly a smurftastrophe!

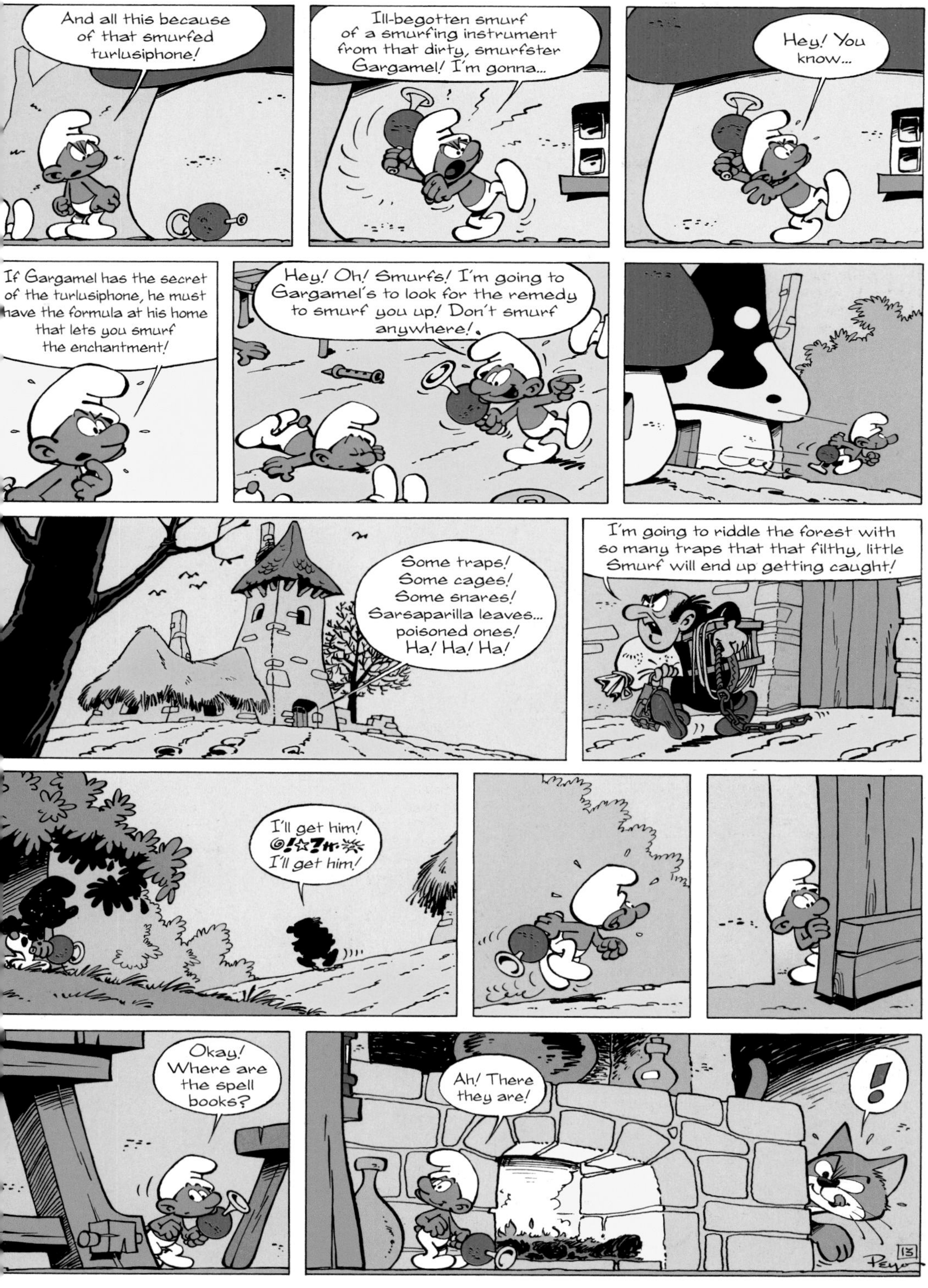
And all this because of that smurfed turlusiphone!
Ill-begotten smurf of a smurfing instrument from that dirty, smurfster Gargamel! I'm gonna...
Hey! You know...
If Gargamel has the secret of the turlusiphone, he must have the formula at his home that lets you smurf the enchantment!
Hey! Oh! Smurfs! I'm going to Gargamel's to look for the remedy to smurf you up! Don't smurf anywhere!
Some traps! Some cages! Some snares! Sarsaparilla leaves... poisoned ones! Ha! Ha! Ha!
I'm going to riddle the forest with so many traps that that filthy, little Smurf will end up getting caught!
I'll get him!
I'll get him!
Okay! Where are the spell books?
Ah! There they are!
!

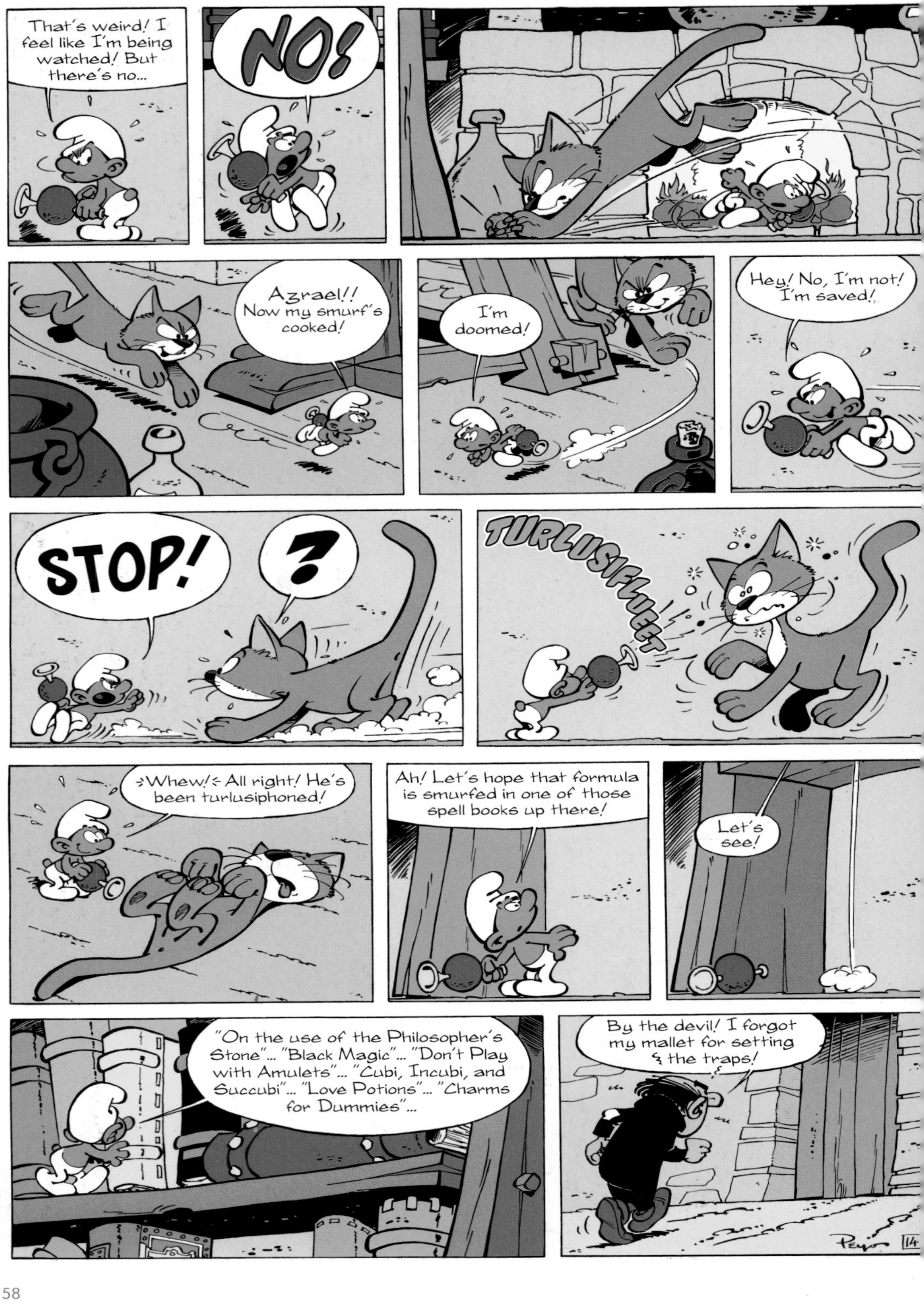

That's weird! I feel like I'm being watched! But there's no...
NO!
Azrael!! Now my smurf's cooked!
I'm doomed!
Hey! No, I'm not! I'm saved!
STOP!
?
TURLUSIFLUET
Whew! All right! He's been turlusiphoned!
Ah! Let's hope that formula is smurfed in one of those spell books up there!
Let's see!
"On the use of the Philosopher's Stone"... "Black Magic"... "Don't Play with Amulets"... "Cubi, Incubi, and Succubi"... "Love Potions"... "Charms for Dummies"...
By the devil! I forgot my mallet for setting the traps!
Peyo
14

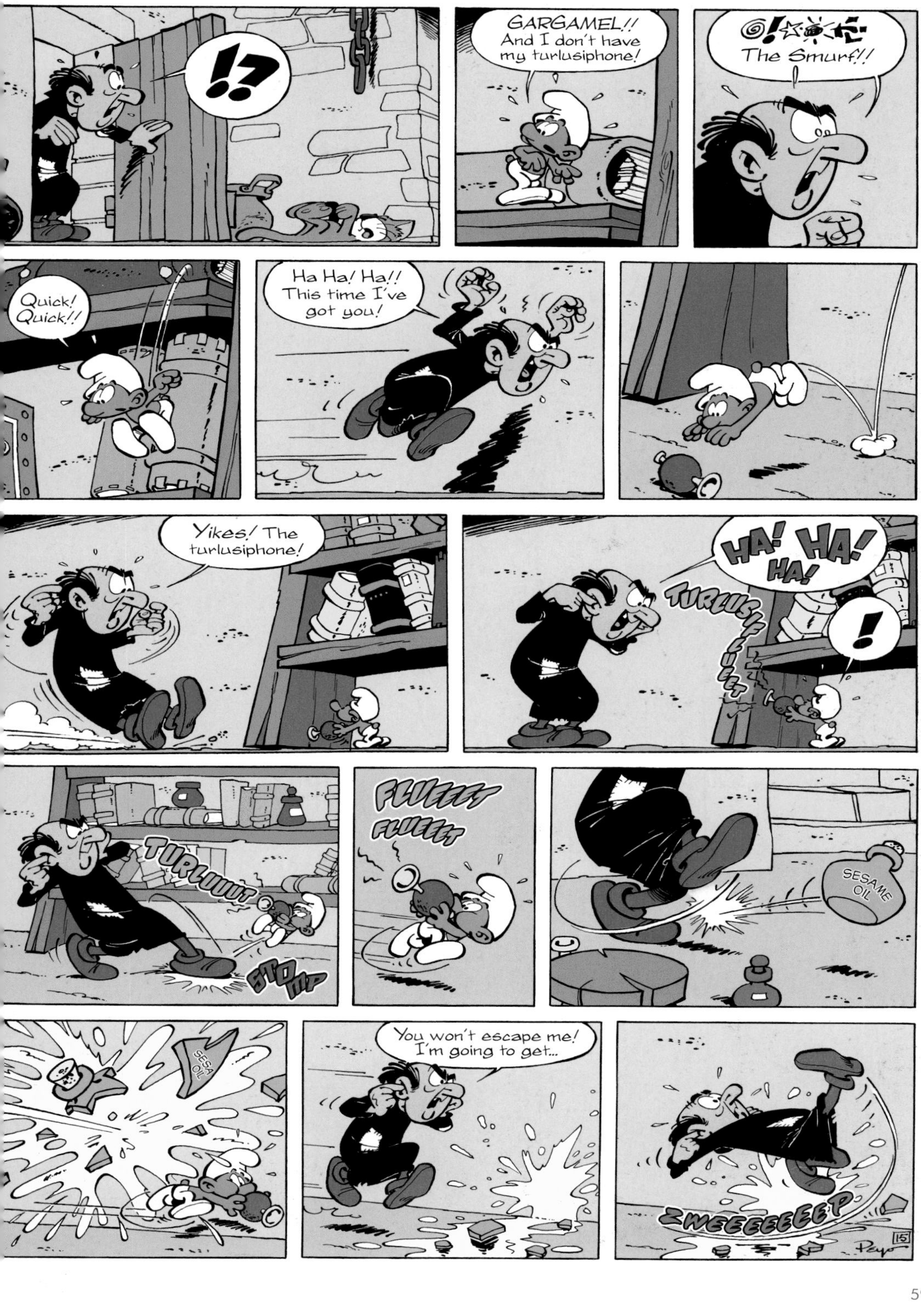
!?
GARGAMEL!! And I don't have my turlusiphone!
The Smurf!!
Quick! Quick!!
Ha Ha! Ha!! This time I've got you!
Yikes! The turlusiphone!
HA! HA! HA!
TURLUSIFLUEET
!
TURLUUUT
STOMP
FLUEEET
FLUEEET
SESAME OIL
SESA OIL
You won't escape me! I'm going to get...
ZWEEEEEEEEP
15
Peyo

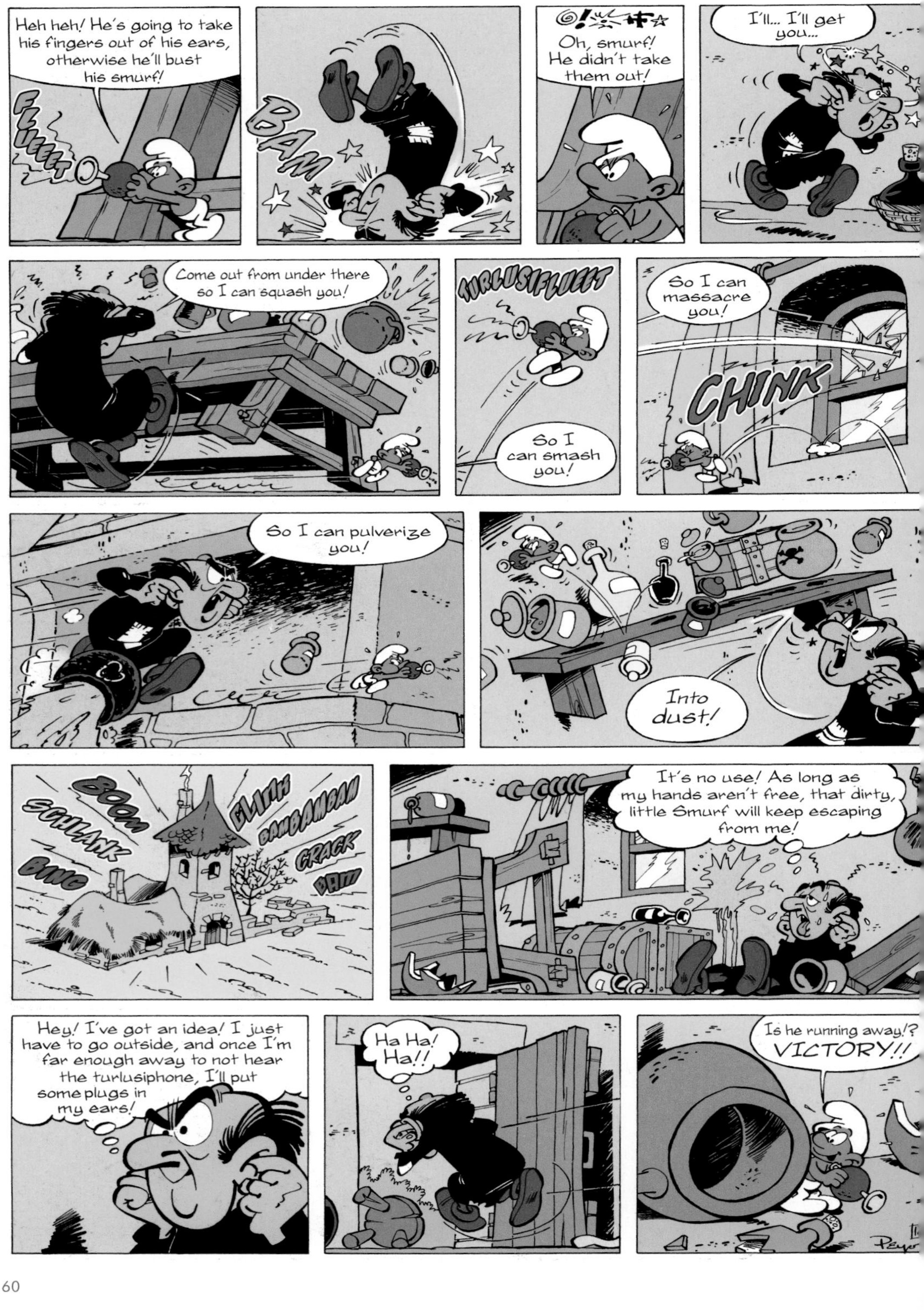

Heh heh! He's going to take his fingers out of his ears, otherwise he'll bust his smurf!
BAM
Oh, smurf! He didn't take them out!
I'll... I'll get you...
Come out from under there so I can squash you!
So I can smash you!
So I can massacre you!
CHINK
So I can pulverize you!
Into dust!
BOOM
BING
CRACK
It's no use! As long as my hands aren't free, that dirty, little Smurf will keep escaping from me!
Hey! I've got an idea! I just have to go outside, and once I'm far enough away to not hear the turlusiphone, I'll put some plugs in my ears!
Ha Ha! Ha!!
Is he running away!? VICTORY!!

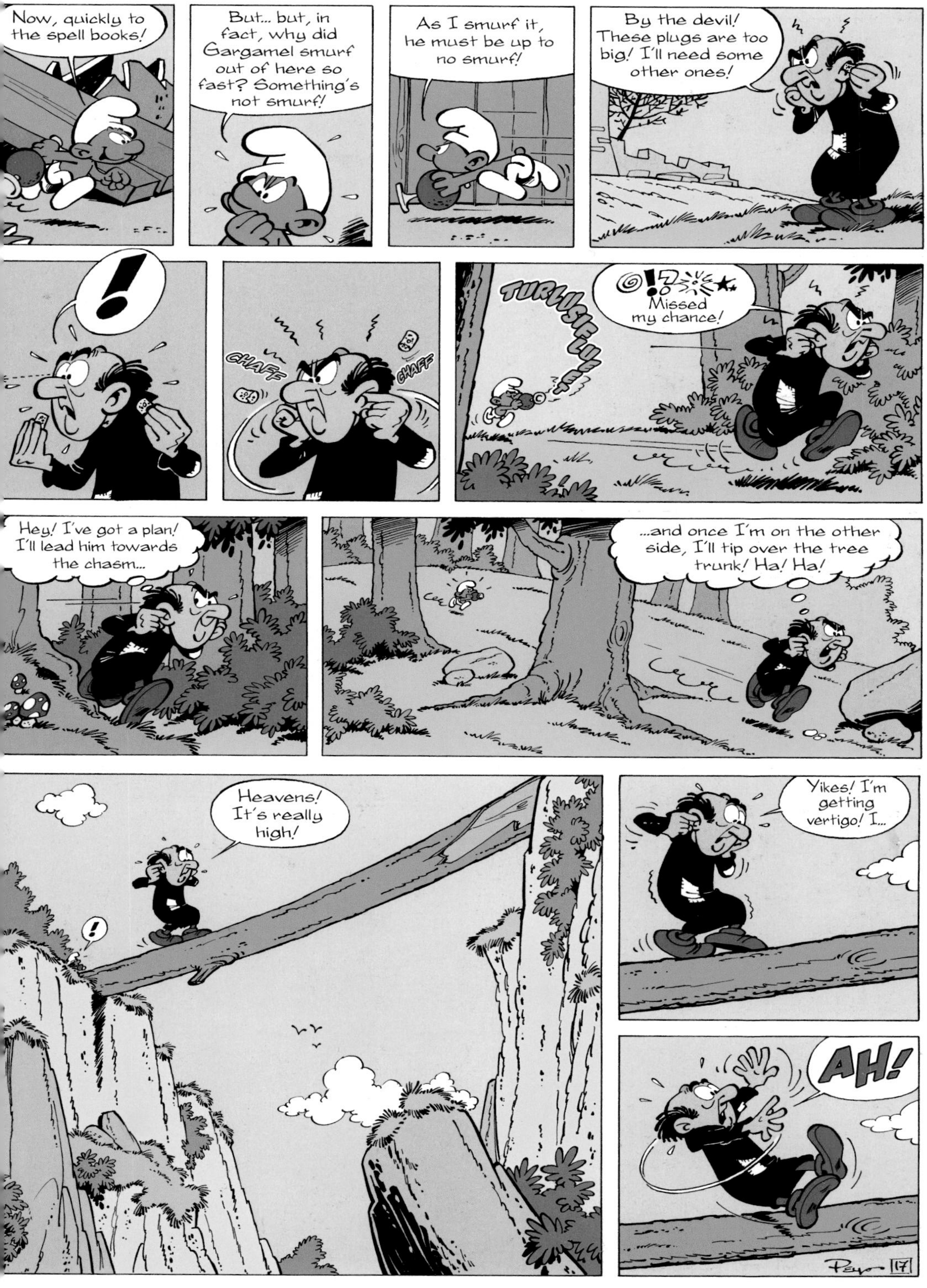

Now, quickly to the spell books!
But... but, in fact, why did Gargamel smurf out of here so fast? Something's not smurf!
As I smurf it, he must be up to no smurf!
By the devil! These plugs are too big! I'll need some other ones!
!
CHAFF
CHAFF
TURLUSIFLUTE
Missed my chance!
Hey! I've got a plan! I'll lead him towards the chasm...
...and once I'm on the other side, I'll tip over the tree trunk! Ha! Ha!
Heavens! It's really high!
!
Yikes! I'm getting vertigo! I...
AH!
Peyo 17

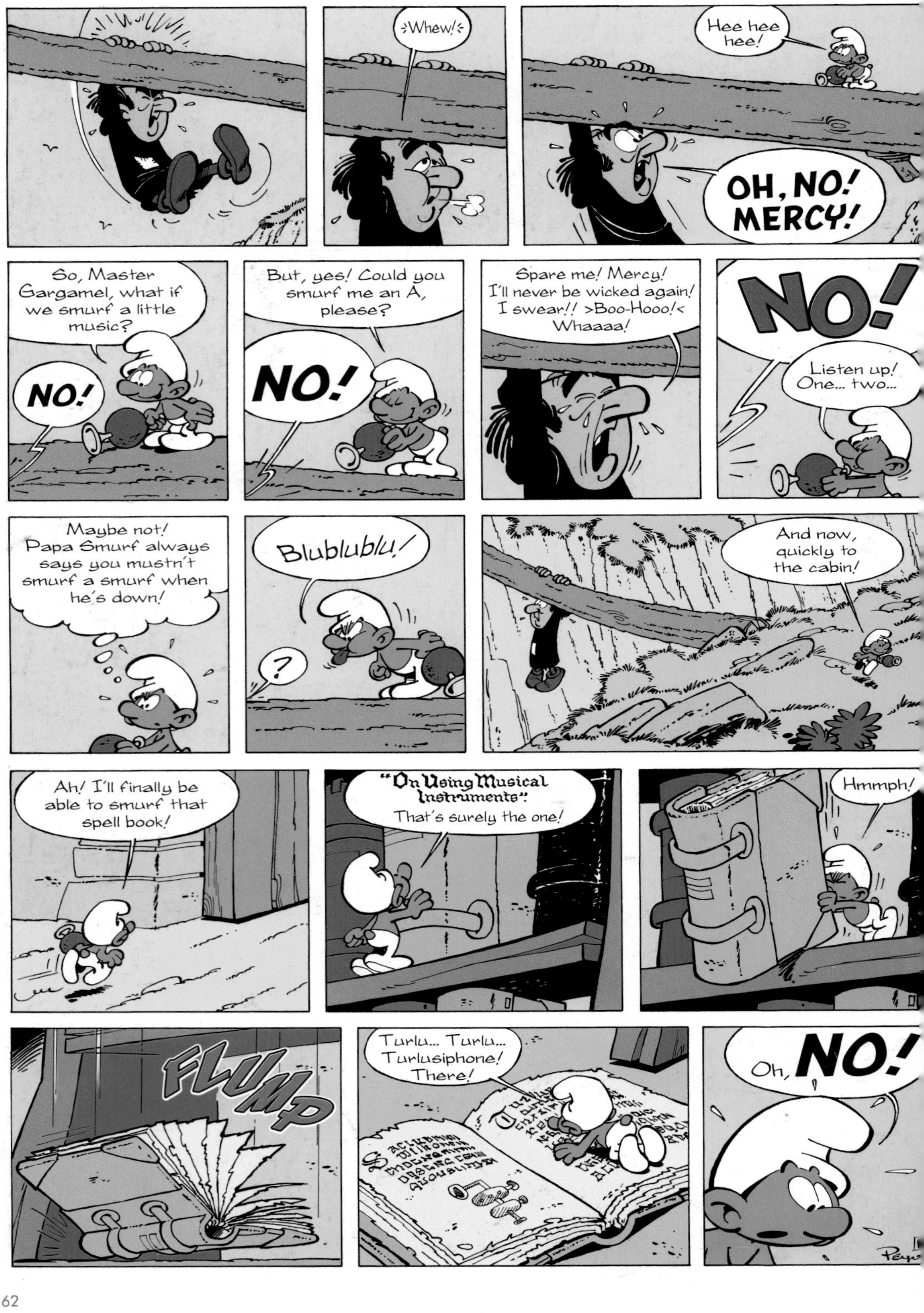
Whew!
Hee hee hee!
OH, NO! MERCY!
So, Master Gargamel, what if we smurf a little music?
NO!
But, yes! Could you smurf me an A, please?
NO!
Spare me! Mercy! I'll never be wicked again! I swear!! >Boo-Hooo!< Whaaaa!
NO!
Listen up! One... two...
Maybe not! Papa Smurf always says you mustn't smurf a smurf when he's down!
Blublublu!
?
And now, quickly to the cabin!
Ah! I'll finally be able to smurf that spell book!
"On Using Musical Instruments": That's surely the one!
Hmmph!
FLUMP
Turlu... Turlu... Turlusiphone! There!
Oh, NO!

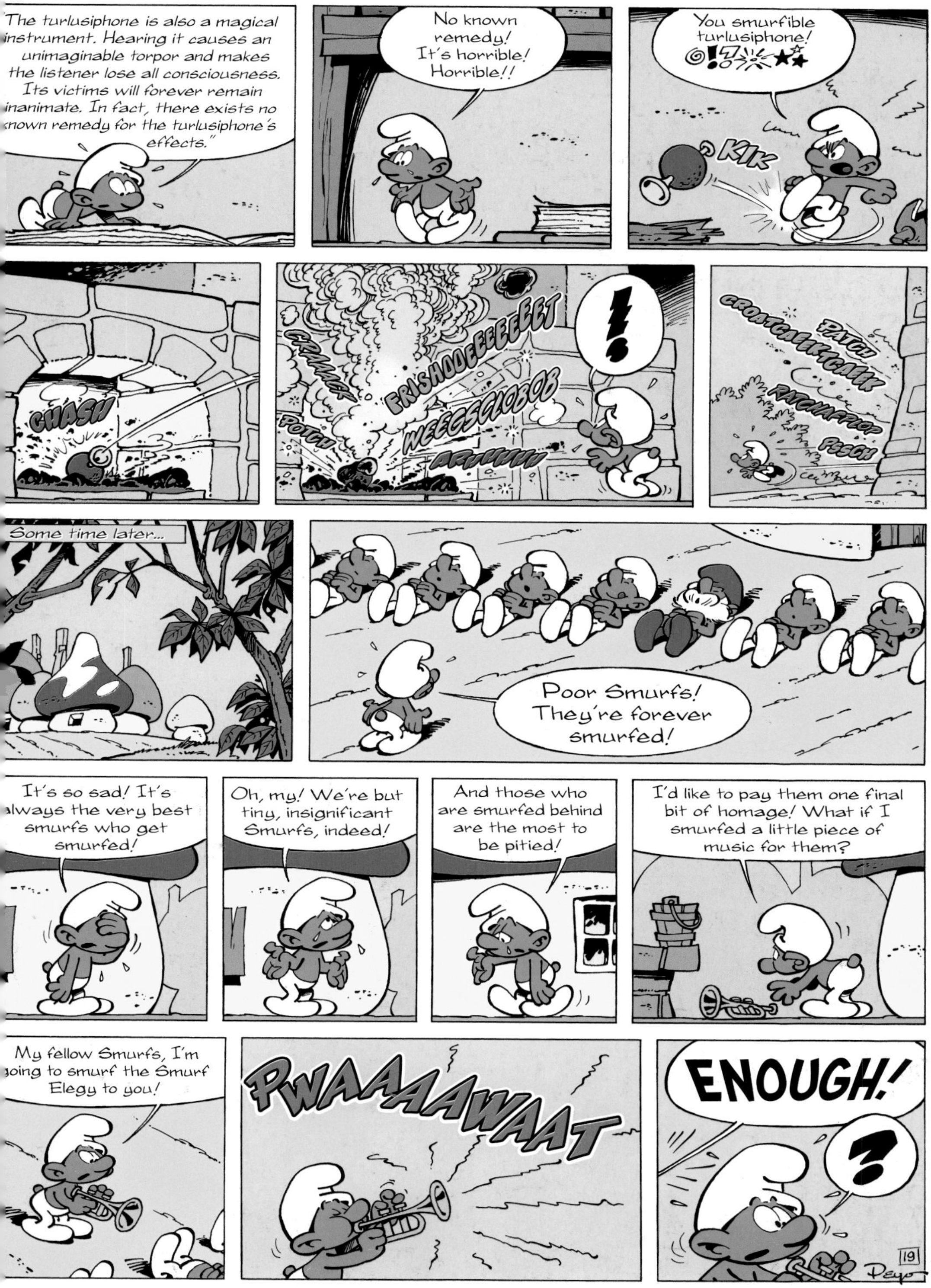

"The turlusiphone is also a magical instrument. Hearing it causes an unimaginable torpor and makes the listener lose all consciousness. Its victims will forever remain inanimate. In fact, there exists no known remedy for the turlusiphone's effects."
No known remedy! It's horrible! Horrible!!
You smurfible turlusiphone!
KIK
CHASH
GRAAAACK
FRISHOOEEEEEEEEET
POTCH
WEEGSCLOBOB
!
CROATCAEEKTCAEEK
PATCH
RATCHAFFLOP
PSSCH
Some time later...
Poor Smurfs! They're forever smurfed!
It's so sad! It's always the very best smurfs who get smurfed!
Oh, my! We're but tiny, insignificant Smurfs, indeed!
And those who are smurfed behind are the most to be pitied!
I'd like to pay them one final bit of homage! What if I smurfed a little piece of music for them?
My fellow Smurfs, I'm going to smurf the Smurf Elegy to you!
PWAAAAAWAAT
ENOUGH!
?
19
Peyo

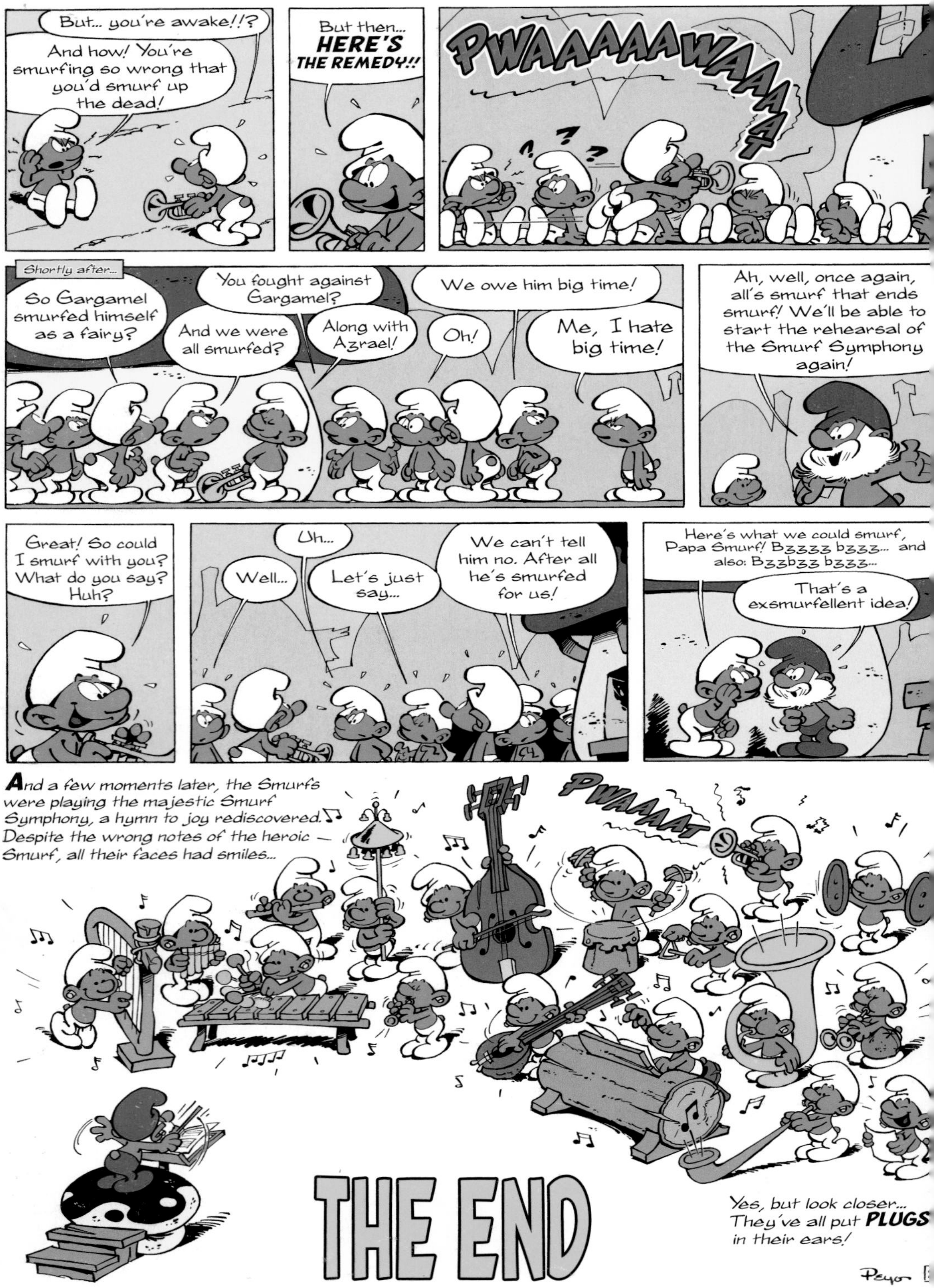

But... you're awake!!?
And how! You're smurfing so wrong that you'd smurf up the dead!
But then... **HERE'S THE REMEDY!!**
PWAAAAAAWAAAAAT
Shortly after...
So Gargamel smurfed himself as a fairy?
You fought against Gargamel?
And we were all smurfed?
Along with Azrael!
We owe him big time!
Oh!
Me, I hate big time!
Ah, well, once again, all's smurf that ends smurf! We'll be able to start the rehearsal of the Smurf Symphony again!
Great! So could I smurf with you? What do you say? Huh?
Uh...
Well...
Let's just say...
We can't tell him no. After all he's smurfed for us!
Here's what we could smurf, Papa Smurf! Bzzzz bzzz... and also: Bzzbzz bzzz...
That's a exsmurfellent idea!
And a few moments later, the Smurfs were playing the majestic Smurf Symphony, a hymn to joy rediscovered. Despite the wrong notes of the heroic Smurf, all their faces had smiles...
PWAAAAT
THE END
Yes, but look closer... They've all put **PLUGS** in their ears!
Peyo